Judd's eyes narrowed. 'Let me get this clear,' he said, a steely thread entering his voice. 'You're ordering me to leave?'

A specialist in calm control, he had rarely lost his temper in the past, and yet whenever the fuse of his anger had been lit the explosion had been severe, volcanic, mind-blazing. Alyson stood a little straighter. She refused to feel threatened. The days of being an unsure, obligingly submissive girl were over.

Books you will enjoy
by ELIZABETH OLDFIELD

FLAWED HERO

Though a lifelong landlubber, Abby had no choice but to start running a temporary day cruise business on the *Calinargo*, her aunt's boat. She knew she would have some local difficulties, but she hadn't anticipated that one of them would be Josh Donner, owner of the only rival firm on the island!

AN ACCIDENTAL AFFAIR

Where women were concerned, journalist Leith Montgomery spelled danger—which didn't bother Sian because she was just a hard-working colleague who was used to hitting the world's hot spots at Leith's side. But their assignment in Chile was different. Was Sian losing her immunity to Leith's charms? And what game was he playing?

BACKLASH

BY

ELIZABETH OLDFIELD

MILLS & BOON LIMITED
ETON HOUSE 18-24 PARADISE ROAD
RICHMOND SURREY TW9 1SR

First published in Great Britain 1991
by Mills & Boon Limited

This edition 1991

ISBN 0 263 77127 X

Set in Times Roman 12 on 12¼ pt.
01-9106-40845 C

Made and printed in Great Britain

CHAPTER ONE

THERE was an intruder in the house!

As if mesmerised, Alyson stared through the drawing-room window, then she blinked and backed hastily down the grassy bank to lurk out of sight behind the blossomed shelter of a luxuriant hydrangea. Her heart hammered in alarm. The glimpse of a retreating shadow in the hall explained the front door's stubborn refusal to unlock and why, when she had rung the bell, there had been no answer. As arranged, her clients had left for their holiday mid-afternoon, and in the meagre two-hour gap someone had broken in—must have done, because apart from the Browns and herself no one else had keys. Alyson frowned. She knew robbery of country residences had become a major growth industry in recent years—much of her business was generated in response—but she had had no idea the crimes were committed with such sneakily expert timing.

Regrets flooded in. If only a person-to-person take-over had been possible. If only Bridie, usually one of her most reliable employees, had not asked for time off at the last moment, leaving her short-staffed and in a fix. If only the break-in did not feel as if it was her fault. Alyson straightened her shoulders. This was foolishness. When she had telephoned yesterday to advise of a delay, the fussy Mrs Brown had been content, and besides, one of Homeminders' clauses clearly stated that during daylight hours property could be left empty for up to three hours. The fact that someone had chosen to steal in *now* was sheer bad luck and coincidence.

So—what did she do? If the sound of her Datsun swinging on to the gravelled drive had failed to penetrate, the clarion call of the bell must have alerted the burglar to her presence. The beat of her heart accelerated. When she had peeped in through the window, had he been peeping out? Alyson wondered. Had he seen her? Was he under the impression she had seen him—clearly—and, if so, what did he intend to do about it? Panic bubbled in her chest. Today's trend was towards increasing violence where people not only had their possessions purloined, they were sometimes killed! Gruesome headlines printed themselves across her mind—'Blonde disturbs thief and is bludgeoned to death in garden.' Yet perhaps it was *thieves*? A single indistinct shape might have been all she had seen, but others could skulk indoors. Several others. 'Blonde gang-raped and bludgeoned' the headline re-wrote itself.

Alyson took a deep breath. Although she had been blessed—or was it shackled?—with a vivid imagination, experience had taught the dangers of allowing it to run riot, and now she ordered herself to keep calm. Common sense said that, as no vehicle had been parked in the lane nor on the frontage to the house, the thief, like most, would be a small-fry opportunist who had happened to amble past and decided to load himself up with as many items of value as he could carry.

Abruptly, a movement beyond the screen of leaves caught her eye. Someone had entered the drawing-room. She peered forward, but summer sunshine had painted the window with reflection and made it difficult to see. Damn! Knowing the kind of villain she was up against would be a definite advantage. Using the flowering bushes as cover, Alyson pushed stealthily up to locate a precarious foothold near the top of the slope but to one side. Cautiously, she squinted out between the branches. Cottonwool clouds filled the uppermost portion of the glass and obscured the intruder's head, but as he strolled over to take a leisurely look out she had an unrestricted view from his shoulders down. Her lips parted in astonishment, her hazel eyes boggled. Apart from a damp towel slung casually around his neck, the intruder was naked.

Her concentration shot, Alyson wobbled, her foot slipped, and in silent confusion she tumbled backwards—clutching and slithering—to end up sprawled inelegantly amid the shrubbery. Winded, she lay there, and when she next looked the window was empty. Brushing earth from the seat of her pewter-grey trousers, she scrambled to her feet. A reappraisal was required. Unless the *modus operandi* had changed, thieves were not in the habit of stripping themselves before they stripped houses, so had Mr Brown given the Warwick trip the thumbs-down at the last moment? Could Gary, the doted-on offspring who was supposed to be backpacking through France, have returned home? Alyson plucked blades of grass from the ivory-coloured blouse she wore beneath a grey suede waistcoat. On both counts, the answer appeared to be 'no'. Mr Brown would be of a similar age to his plump, bespectacled wife, which made him around fifty, while his son was still in his teens. But, with rippling muscles, taut stomach and lean hips, the tanned figure had been that of someone in his thirties—at a guess.

There needed to be an element of guesswork, Alyson thought wryly, for it was a long time since an undressed man had wandered into her sights—and even longer since she had watched one so at ease in his own body. With square-tipped fingers spread on his hips as he surveyed the garden, the intruder *had* been easy. Her thoughts flew back. Once she had been attached to a male who had possessed a similarly nonchalant approach to nudity. A male whose nonchalance had extended to rubbish bins and sex and marriage. A male who—— She scowled at a scratch on her arm. Why was she thinking of him now?

The intruder must be a vagrant who had been mooching in the vicinity, noticed the Browns loading suitcases into their car, and identified a chance to partake of the good life, Alyson decided. On balance, this seemed preferable to a burglar, though only just; for, while looting might not be an issue, damage could be caused to the home which Mrs Brown had been exceedingly anxious to protect. Her hazel eyes sparked. The towel and stray droplets of water which had dappled his skin indicated that the man had recently emerged from the shower. He had wasted no time settling in, she thought indignantly. How dared he use one of the squeaky-clean bathrooms with their floral tiling and sunken tubs and spotlit mirrors? How dared he pad around on the thick pale carpets? How dared he install himself as master of a house which, for the next fortnight, was *her* responsibility! Alyson powered off around the corner. Mr Adonis must be removed before he could insinuate himself even further.

But as she neared the front porch, her stride slowed. Much as her preference was to turf him out immediately and curtail any damage, summoning the police rated as a wiser course of action. There would be a delay while she went to fetch them, yet not only was it essential from the business angle that the break-in be put on record—if anything had been harmed, the Browns and their insurance company must know Homeminders was not responsible—but tackling him herself could be risky. Alyson stopped dead. When instructed to depart, the vagrant would doubtless become abusive, but he had looked fearsomely fit and strong, so he might also, if it suited him, inflict injury. All of a sudden, she remembered Rio, the Great Dane which had barked loud and long on her preliminary visit. Mrs Brown claimed that the dog made an excellent deterrent, so where was it now? How had the man managed to silence an animal that equalled the size of a small pony? How, if he realised she was alert to his illegal occupation, might he decide to silence her? Nervously she glanced around. The converted oast-house might nestle in the lush folds of the East Sussex hills and come equipped with idyllic gardens and swimming pool, but it was a good mile from any neighbour and six from the nearest town.

Her stride switched to a furtive tiptoe. She must leave, and fast. As she crept towards the Datsun, Alyson slid the key from her hip pocket and held it poised at the ready. The forecourt was wide, she comforted herself, so all she needed to do was jump in, swing the car around, and shoot down the drive and out through the stone gateposts to safety. Simple. With head bent and heavy strands of wheat-gold hair falling forward to half cover her face, she was inserting the key when, behind her, the front door suddenly opened. The breath caught in her throat. Someone had stepped out on to the porch, and that someone must have seen her. Alyson's fingers thickened into rubber thumbs. Unlocking the car became a tricky operation.

'Hey!' a male voice called.

She took no notice. Escape was all. Feverishly, the key was turned, the handle tugged, and she had wrenched open the door when a large hand landed like a clamp on her shoulder. Her blood ran cold. Fear snaked down her spine. She had been caught. She was trapped. The intruder had her at his mercy.

'Hey,' the voice said again, softer this time and questioning.

A second hand covered her other shoulder and she was manoeuvred around to face him. Her nerves a-jangle, Alyson looked fearfully up. The man had thick dark hair, piercing pale blue eyes and a blunt, chiselled jaw. In a light-headed moment of shock, she gasped. Her captor was Judd Hamilton, her ex-husband!

CHAPTER TWO

THEIR eyes met and locked, and for what seemed an eternity they stared at each other.

'Well, well, if it isn't the alluring Alyson,' Judd said at last.

'What—what are you doing here?' she asked, attempting to struggle free from the tangle of emotions which, like a net over a butterfly, had enmeshed her.

'I'm a house guest.'

'You can't be!'

'Yep. I'm staying from today, Friday, for a week.' He began buttoning the short-sleeved black and white striped shirt which, with a pair of worn jeans, had obviously been thrown on. 'Mike passed over a set of spare keys and told me to make myself at home, which I've been doing for the past hour. You remember Mike Brown? We used to work together.'

Alyson's mind reeled back to the City office where, in what seemed like another age, she had first set eyes on Judd, who was a high-powered, highly skilled, highly rewarded foreign exchange dealer—an occupation which allowed him to indulge the buccaneering aspect of his character with impunity.

'Gwen Brown is married to—to that Mr Brown?' she stammered, recalling a pleasant, if somewhat taciturn man with a grey stubble haircut and a prominent nose. He had held a position on the managerial side.

'I've never met his wife, but her name is Gwendolen and this is where they live.'

'So far from London?' she protested.

The shirt was rammed into his jeans. 'Mike commutes by car. It takes around ninety minutes each way, much to his annoyance.'

'Mrs Brown wasn't aware you were coming,' Alyson said tartly.

He cast her a puzzled look. 'You know the woman?' he queried.

'Not well, but I called here earlier in the week and she told me then that absolutely no guests were expected.'

Judd lifted a broad shoulder into a shrug. 'It's possible she wasn't informed. Mike can be vague, but also I get the impression that he and his better half are involved in a running skirmish these days and don't share too much by way of communication.'

Alyson closed the car door. In the first year and a half of their marriage, she and Judd had communicated like crazy. Yet in the final months, the months when everything had fallen apart, they had been like strangers who each spoke a different language.

'I'm sorry, but you'll need to alter your plans,' she said.

'Excuse me?'

'The impression *I* got is that the house is very much Gwen Brown's domain, and even if her husband did issue an invitation I'm sure she'd never agree to a stranger taking up residence during her absence. She's extremely fastidious.'

Judd's eyes narrowed. 'Let me get this clear,' he said, a steely thread entering his voice, 'you're ordering me to leave?'

A specialist in calm control, he had rarely lost his temper in the past, and yet whenever the fuse of his anger had been lit the explosion had been severe, volcanic, mind-blasting. Alyson stood a little straighter. She refused to feel threatened. The days of being an unsure, obligingly submissive girl were over.

'I'm asking.' She scissored a smile. 'Please.'

Judd brushed strands of dark hair from his brow. 'You're extraordinary!' he rasped. 'After three years we finally bump into each other and in two seconds flat I'm being told to beat it. Whatever happened to—are you well, Judd? What have you been doing recently? How are your folks? I don't expect to be clasped to your bosom in joyous delight,' he added, his eyes flashing insolently down to her breasts, 'but some recognition that we were once joined together in holy matrimony would be appropriate. Go?' he stampeded on. 'Why the hell should I? My visit has nothing whatsoever to do with you, and why you should imagine you have any right to——'

'I do have the right,' Alyson broke in determinedly. 'I run a company called Homeminders which provides a residential caretaking service for people who are reluctant to leave their houses empty while they're away, and Mrs Brown has engaged us.'

His thick black brows compressed. 'You mean you're scheduled to move in here?'

'For two weeks. As well as guarding against thieves and vandals, we also eliminate the chore of closing up the house and will look after any pets,' she rattled off, quoting her brochure as though it provided additional justification for her presence. She hesitated. 'What's happened to the dog?' she asked, abruptly reminded.

'He's dozing in his basket in the utility-room. He barked a couple of times when I arrived, but tickle him behind the ears and he's a big softie.' Judd thrust his hands deep into the pockets of his jeans, stretching the faded denim tight across his thighs. 'Mike may have suggested I shack up here out of bloody-mindedness because he knew his wife wouldn't approve,' he said, returning to the fray, 'but the guy is allowed to invite his own friends to his own home.' He shot a glance at the oast-house. 'After all, it's his hard-earned cash which has paid for this splendour.'

Alyson wrinkled her nose. 'I reckon it's *too* splendid. Mrs Brown took me on a guided tour, and every room looked so arranged, so colour-co-ordinated, so perfect.'

'You were very into perfection yourself once,' he remarked.

Alyson frowned. 'Was I? Maybe,' she agreed, then pushed the thought away. 'But living here will be like living in one of those show houses at an Ideal Home exhibition, so it's not the ideal environment for a holiday,' she declared. 'I assume a holiday is the reason you're here?'

Judd hesitated. 'Not exactly.'

'Whatever,' she dismissed, 'there are plenty of other places in the area where you can base yourself, places where you'll be able to relax. Why not try a hotel in Battle? There are a couple of olde-worlde ones which are easy-going and full of charm. The town's charming too, and interesting. The Abbey there was built to commemorate 1066 and the Battle of Hastings when William of Normandy and Harold——'

'Thanks, but I don't require a history lesson,' Judd interjected, 'and I shan't be booking into any hotel. I'm staying put, *in situ*, *here*.'

'You can't!' Alyson protested, her voice rising in a hoarse, scratchy squeak.

'I bloody am, and would you kindly stop telling me what I can and can't do. You never used to act the boss lady,' he grated, flinging her an accusing look. 'You've changed.'

You haven't, she thought uneasily. You're just as self-possessed, as determined, as forceful as ever. And as attractive. Although Judd's features were too strong and angular for him to fall into the 'handsome' category, the intense blue of his eyes and the liquid ease with which he moved ensured a personal magnetism and made him compulsive to watch. He had presence.

'Mrs Brown has employed Homeminders to——' Alyson started earnestly, but he was there first.

'Someone told me you'd set up in business, though they didn't know what line. How do you enjoy being an entrepreneur?' he enquired.

'Very much. As much as Sophia did,' she heard herself add, and immediately wondered what perversity had made her mention the woman who, in what now seemed a fine irony, had once been her role model. A few months before she and Judd had separated, her connection with Sophia had been severed and, as with her former spouse, thoughts of the svelte brunette had been locked away in a box in her head. It was a box she preferred not to open, yet all of a sudden memories were spilling out—painful memories. Alyson's winged brows came low. Her mind seemed to be operating on several levels at once. The past, the present, and the immediate future—in the form of how did she persuade Judd to depart?—were mingled up together.

'How long has your company been in operation?' he asked.

'Coming up to two years.'

'Is trade good?'

'Too good,' she replied, 'which is why I'm here. I don't normally home-sit myself, but one of my ladies wanted to visit a new granddaughter, so——'

'You sent her off with your best wishes' said Judd, when she spread her hands. 'That's not like Sophia.'

'No,' Alyson agreed, privately admitting that in letting Bridie go on the spur of the moment she might have been unprofessional and a little too compliant. But how could she refuse when the woman had been so eager to see the latest addition to her family?

'There was no one else who could take her place?' he queried.

'Unfortunately not. This summer every member of the team's been fully utilised and I need to recruit more, but if someone is putting their house in your care it's imperative that whoever takes charge is trustworthy. I look for conscientious, responsible people and demand references from doctors, solicitors, JPs, and check them thoroughly, but it all takes time, and for months now time's been in short supply. I'm way behind with my accounts and tax return, and the truth is I need a partner. But I'll get by,' she finished, abruptly aware of being overly talkative and too revealing.

Why she should be telling him this, Alyson did not know. Although they had shared almost everything else in the past, the one thing she had never shared with Judd were her problems. At the time, it had seemed like a confession of ineptitude, though, in retrospect, her silence could be recognised as youthful insecurity.

'Especially if you spend the next week at your office,' Judd said.

'Sorry?'

'There's no necessity for you to stay here, not yet. I'm willing to look after House Beautiful and the dog for the next seven days. Why don't we have a drink,' he suggested, gesturing that they should go indoors, 'and you can fill me in on what's required before you leave?'

Alyson walked ahead of him into the wide hall, but as they reached the spacious cottage-style kitchen with its 'antique' finished wood units and shelves of burnished copperware, she spun round to confront him.

'I'm not leaving,' she said.

Judd frowned. 'I thought you wanted to get to grips with your paperwork?'

'I do, which is why I've brought some of it with me.'

'You'd be far better off if you had all your files around you.'

'True,' she conceded. 'However, my receptionist's at the office in Hampstead, so if I should require any additional information I can ring and ask.'

Judd shot her an irritated look. If she was anxious for him to push off so, it seemed, he also wanted to see the back of her. She did not blame him. Their parting might have been as amicable as it had been possible to achieve in the circumstances, yet it represented failure—and he thrived on success.

'Tea or coffee?' he asked.

'Coffee, and I'll make it,' said Alyson, stepping quickly past to plug in the huge white filter machine which, like her plethora of state-of-the-art gadgets, Mrs Brown had gloated over at length.

Judd rested a hip against the scrubbed pine table. 'I am capable of preparing a couple of cups of coffee and I can occupy a house without anything coming to grief. *I'm* trustworthy,' he said heavily.

'Is that so?' Hand-crafted earthenware mugs were unhooked from the mug tree. 'Who was it who forgot about his cigarette and almost set fire to our flat? Who was it who allowed the bath to overflow?'

'One, I've stopped smoking, and——'

'You have?' she chipped in, surprised because dealing was a matter of cut-and-thrust, pumping adrenalin and quick decisions, and he had always maintained that if he was to function effectively his packet a day was essential.

'Not had a cigarette all year,' he replied, 'and, two, the bathroom flooded because——' Judd's blue eyes stapled themselves to hers '—when I came out to fetch fresh clothes you trailed a finger along my thigh and we became involved in some very engrossing, very time-consuming, very hot sex.'

Alyson flushed, tardily acknowledging that the soaked carpet had been as much her fault as his. Another of Judd's assertions, she remembered, had been that their frequent lovemaking was a vital factor in soothing away the strains and stresses. It had had her purring, she thought, in reluctant nostalgia.

'I'll admit we were often in danger of catching bubonic plague before I got around to taking out the rubbish,' he continued, 'but——' a long-fingered hand was raised '—I swear on oath that my removal of such is now immaculate and immediate.'

'Since when?' she asked, in scornful disbelief.

'Since I've been looking after myself. Knowing the buck—and the muck—stops with you concentrates the mind beautifully.'

'Mrs Brown has paid the fee in advance, so it's my duty to be here,' Alyson said doggedly.

'All that matters is having someone around,' Judd returned, 'and if a man in a balaclava did call with the intention of filching the silver I'd be far more capable of apprehending him.' He tilted a sardonic head. 'Unless these assertiveness training weekends you've obviously been attending have resulted in you becoming a black belt at karate?'

'It was agreed I'd take charge and I will!' she insisted.

'You want us to cohabit?' he drawled.

Her heart gave a lurch. 'Of course not! What a stupid thing to say. You think I'm angling to stay because you're here? You must be out of your mind. Huh, I——'

'Methinks the lady doth protest too much,' Judd murmured, his smile careless and mocking.

Alyson clenched her fists. 'Methinks she wants the gentleman to vamoose and this house to be looked after by someone who's neat and tidy!'

He stretched out a hand and untangled a piece of hydrangea from her shoulder-length bob of dark blonde hair.

'Being festooned with twigs isn't tidy,' he remarked.

His touch possessed all the impact of an electric shock and Alyson reared back. She did not care if she was plastered from head to foot in debris, she objected to this invasion of her personal space. Their days of physical contact were past, gone, finished.

'I fell over—and I hurt my arm. It was your fault!' she declared.

Judd twirled the twig in his fingers. 'Mine?'

'I tried to open the front door, and when I couldn't I rang the bell,' she began to explain.

'I heard it, but I was under the shower.'

'So I gathered, when you strolled into the drawing-room.'

'You saw me?' His brows rose. 'I thought I'd caught sight of something, but it took a moment to sink in and when I came back to investigate whatever it was appeared to have gone.'

'I'd decided to scout around, noticed a shadow and—and took a look,' she said, her voice petering awkwardly off as she visualised again what she had seen.

Judd smiled. 'Peeping Tom is alive and well—and has remembered I take my coffee with a dash of milk and one sugar.'

Alyson stared down, amazed—and infuriated—to discover that after three years apart she had automatically prepared the drink the way he liked it. She thrust the mug at him. She might have pampered Judd in the past, but there was no reason to do so now.

'I was not peeping!' she defended heatedly. 'I might have been standing in the bushes, but——'

'The frustrations of solitary living haven't inspired a fetish for spying on naked men?' he enquired.

'Although I live alone, that doesn't mean I'm sex-starved,' Alyson declared, with more vigour than regard for truth.

'I haven't heard talk of you having a lover,' Judd remarked, and tasted his coffee. 'Not recently.'

'Perhaps your ear hasn't been close enough to the ground,' she retorted. 'I'd noticed a movement in the hall and you came to the window, but I couldn't see your head, only your body and——'

'You never realised you were gawking at your one-time husband? You didn't recognise the manly attributes which used to provide you with so much pleasure?'

Colour filled her cheeks. '—and it was such a shock to find the house occupied—by a flasher,' Alyson inserted caustically, 'that I lost my balance.'

'In other words, I bowled you over,' said Judd, his smile tipping into a grin. 'I know playing more sport has made me fitter, but I never realised one look at my Ramboesque physique would turn your knees to jelly, knock you head over heels, make you——'

'In other words, I thought you were a tramp!' she snapped.

'How to go from hero to zero,' he muttered.

'Pardon me?'

'When we walked down the aisle you thought I was a god; now I'm mistaken for a bum.'

Alyson took a restorative sip of coffee. 'I'm sorry to wreck your arrangements, but you have only just moved in, so moving out isn't going to be that big a hassle, is it?' she appealed. 'I'm sure when you think about it you'll agree it's for the best, and I'm sure you'll be able to fix accommodation elsewhere.'

His blue eyes went cold. 'Are you? I'm not. But stop trying to muscle me,' Judd said tersely, 'it won't work. You might have written me off once, but I'm damned if you'll do it again.'

'Written you off?' she protested, in bewilderment. 'I didn't!'

'No? Well, I don't feel inclined to debate that right now, and neither do I wish to become involved in a fight to the death over where I sleep tonight.' In an angry movement, he hooked out a chair from under the table and straddled it. 'Mike offered me his hospitality and I accepted, and that's that!'

'But——'

'Alyson, it's ended!'

The temptation to argue simmered until, in the face of her continued rebellion, his warning eyes met hers. She sighed. Judd's stare was a weapon in itself, so she temporarily shelved her disagreement, sat down opposite and drank her coffee.

Maybe she should take him up on his offer and leave? Alyson mused. She had no wish to renege on the arrangement with Mrs Brown, yet neither did she have any desire to spend the next seven nights under the same roof as Judd. Grief, if a ten-minute conversation made her this tense and this edgy, what would a week in his company do? Probably turn her into a gibbering idiot. Methodically, she began working her way through a mental checklist. On Monday the dog was to be taken to the kennels for grooming, while on Tuesday she had agreed to change a couple of gerbils from their current cage to a waiting fresh one. The house plants must be watered, phone calls recorded, and the gardener and the pool man allowed access, but Judd could manage that. He would need to make sure that whenever he went out all doors and windows were secured, and be given her number in case of emergencies. Her thoughts ticked on. Whatever disorder he might create, she would have a week to set the house to rights—and her client could be reimbursed with half the fee.

'With regard to Sophia,' Judd said, all of a sudden, 'were you aware that she and Trevor are living in Saudi Arabia?' Alyson shook her head. 'Trevor has a three-year contract as operations chief at an oil field out there.'

'That's why Sophia sold the laundry?' she asked. 'I read about it in the paper.'

'It was sold because she received an offer she dared not refuse,' Judd replied pithily.

Her former employer had triumphed again? It was no surprise. Sophia had done everything with flair—be it running her business, the management of her home, or organising splendid parties. And as a sophisticated 'older' woman, she had also been clever at engaging the interest of younger men, Alyson thought grimly.

'I ran across Trevor when he was visiting his head office a few weeks back and he insisted we have a drink together,' Judd carried on. 'But all he really wanted to do was show me endless photographs of their son.'

Abruptly a band seemed to tighten around her chest, crushing her ribs and cramping her heart.

'Oh,' she said.

'Trevor's a besotted father, though as they spent umpteen years hoping for a child I guess that's to be expected. The kid's two now.'

'He was two in March,' Alyson mumbled.

Judd's brows lifted. 'Is that right? I'm surprised you can remember. I realised he couldn't be a babe in arms any more, but I'd completely lost track.'

'He—he's like Trevor?' she faltered.

'Same sandy hair, same stocky build,' he confirmed. 'A regular chip off the old block.'

Alyson drained her mug. She had known the little boy would look like Trevor, had known it for a long time. A very long time. She gritted her teeth. She was not going to dwell on the past, on what had happened and what she had done. She refused to resurrect her guilty feelings and her regrets.

'Mind you, Trevor's more grey than sandy these days,' Judd continued, 'but he must be almost fifty, and age comes to us all.' He grinned across the table. 'Even to you. It's—what, a month until you hit the big three-o?'

'So?' she said, a touch defensively.

His grin widened. 'So not being able to describe yourself as a young thing any more takes a bit of getting used to, but believe me, it's not that bad.'

At this reminder of her age, Alyson performed an about-turn. In acting as though Judd's presence was—and would be—an earth-shattering event, she had been exhibiting a pathetic lack of maturity, but she was almost thirty and an adult. This meant she would *not* allow his proximity to faze her and she would *not* flee the house like some terror-stricken juvenile. A contract had been signed committing someone from Homeminders to take up residence during the Browns' absence, and reside here she would. She saw no reason to forgo a week's fee on his account!

'Which bedroom are you in?' she enquired, determined that, from now on, her behaviour would be sturdily grown-up.

'The one which overlooks the orchard at the back. Judging from the collection of heavy metal CDs, it's Gary's. Mike said there were four bedrooms and I could use any, apart from the master bedroom.'

'I'll be in what Mrs Brown called the rose room.'

Amusement played around his mouth. 'You're willing to have a stab at peaceful co-existence?'

'Why not?' Alyson said airily. 'Our marriage wasn't that bad. We weren't at loggerheads all the time.'

'We weren't at loggerheads *most* of the time,' Judd replied. 'Where is this rose room?'

'To the left off the landing and up a few stairs. It's at the front of the house.'

There was the subtle arch of a brow. 'Which is as far away from me as possible?'

'Which is where Mrs Brown and I agreed I would sleep,' she rejoined. 'We also agreed that I'd use whatever I need from the freezer and the store cupboard and bill her for anything extra. But now that you're here, I'll make a note of the food and drink which is consumed.'

'And divide everything into his and hers?' Judd enquired drolly.

'It's important for my client's sake that the record is kept straight,' Alyson replied, briskly businesslike. She rose from her chair. 'I'll bring in my things.'

'Can I help?'

About to utter a swift 'no, thanks' and be defiantly independent, she pictured the goods crammed into her car. An impulsive packer who, when in doubt, pushed things in in preference to leaving them out, Alyson had arrived with what, on reflection, seemed a whole flotilla of extraneous items.

'Yes, please.'

As she gathered her raincoat, a couple of jackets, several plastic bags, and her suitcase, Judd carried in the large cardboard box which contained her accounts.

'Where would you like this?' he asked.

'In the study.'

Alyson dumped her load at the foot of the stairs, then hung up the coats in the cloakroom. When she joined him, the documents were on the desk and he was leafing through a novel which he had taken from one of the shelves which lined the large, square room.

'It's a great waste, but I reckon these books are purely decorative,' Judd said, gesturing towards the rows of gold-embossed classics, collections of hefty encyclopaedias, yards of bright-jacketed hardbacks. 'Certainly Mike can't read them; with all his commuting he'd never have the time.'

'Why did he buy this place when it involves him in so much travelling?' Alyson enquired.

'Pressure from the *hausfrau*. Apparently she saw it advertised in an up-market property magazine and fell in love at first sight. I understand it was like something featured in *Homes & Gardens* then, but for seven years she's been making what she insists are refinements. There've been extensions to several rooms, replacement windows, perpetual painting and decorating and renewal of the furnishings.'

'Mrs Brown appears to be stricken with a "country home" mentality,' she remarked, her eyes going from the tan leather-topped desk to the oyster and tan curtains to the oyster-coloured lampshades with their identical tan fringing.

'And how!' Judd turned down his mouth. 'Mike's fed up with her obsession with the house and fed up with the daily drive, and he wants them to move closer to London, but whenever he raises the subject his wife finds something that needs to be done and won't listen.' He replaced the book. 'Did she say anything about their holiday?'

'Only that they're staying at the hotel where they spent their honeymoon. She didn't seem keen. In fact, she told me she'd rather have spent the fortnight at home and it was her husband who'd insisted on going. Do you think he intends to try and persuade her to move while they're away?' Alyson queried.

Judd nodded. 'Mike also said there were a number of other matters that need to be sorted out between them, and they'd do it better if Gwendolen wasn't running around polishing doorknobs or rearranging the furniture.' His shoulders were raised and lowered. 'And if things can't be sorted out, who knows, they might decide on a divorce.'

Dismay struck. 'A—a divorce?' Alyson quavered. 'But while they're in Warwick they celebrate their silver wedding!'

'Whether you've been together twenty-five years or two, it can happen. You should know that,' Judd said brusquely.

She did know. She also knew divorce could occur after six years, which had been the time-scale of her parents' marriage, Alyson thought regretfully. Months after her birth, her father had departed and quickly met the woman who was to become his second wife and give him his second family. This had meant that any meetings had been occasional and brief and that her much longed-for 'daddy' was a virtual stranger.

Judd walked out into the hall and picked up her suitcase. 'I'll deliver this,' he said.

Collecting her other possessions, Alyson followed him up the stairs and across the galleried landing to an officiously feminine room where the curtains were patterned with cabbage roses and there was a preponderance of pale pinks and greens.

'Even though the house is too much of a showplace, it's in a superb location,' Judd remarked, looking out of the window to where the afternoon sun was gilding hedgerows and the acres of cornfields which stretched beyond the lane.

'Gorgeous,' she agreed, 'though I wouldn't fancy being stuck here on my own all day and every day, like Mrs Brown. The son's away at university, so he doesn't need looking after, and yet she insists she's too busy to take a job or even become a member of the local coffee-morning circuit.

'Perhaps it's being on her own so much that's made her so fanatical,' he remarked, and straightened. 'I'll leave you to get unpacked.'

When Alyson had stowed her clothes away, she went over to the window. Elbows on the sill—made from natural ash, so Gwen Brown had proudly informed her—she gazed out at the hills that rolled to the horizon. Apart from the gently waving corn and an occasional bird which soared high, nothing moved. She had decided that it would probably be possible to stand there all day and never see another human being, when a car with a rooftop 'taxi' sign drew to a halt beside the gateposts and a girl in her teens climbed out. Mainly built of long brown legs and swinging flaxen hair, she wore a white off-the-shoulder top, blue denim hot pants which appeared to have been chewed off at the thigh, and white boots. As Alyson watched, she became busy paying off the driver. There could be no doubt that her destination was the oast-house, and the bulky holdall lying on the road beside her indicated that she intended to stay.

Alyson's mouth sketched a tight line. When asked why he was here, Judd, she now remembered, had hesitated and said he was 'not exactly' on holiday, and that remark, allied with the girl's appearance, suddenly opened up a whole new scenario. Ever since their split, she had studiously avoided places where they might come face to face, but had found it impossible to escape mutual acquaintances. Through them she had learned that Judd spent his time escorting a veritable procession of nubile females—and here was yet another. Her hazel eyes blazed. His oh, so emphatic insistence that he would take charge while she absented herself and made inroads into her paperwork—how kind!—had been nothing but a ploy and a smokescreen. The reason he had wanted to get rid of her was that he had arranged to frolic with a girl fresh from the cradle. Alyson headed for the stairs. Tough luck! No way was she going to play gooseberry while her erstwhile soulmate and his infant mistress kissed and cooed.

'Judd?' she called.

'In here.'

Pink-cheeked and indignant, she arrived in the doorway to the study. 'She can't stay,' she announced.

He looked up from a book he was reading. 'Who?'

'The nymphet. Your friend. Her!' she explained, marching over to jab a finger out of the window.

There was a glimpse of the driver waving a fond farewell as the taxi moved away, then the newcomer lifted her bag and began sauntering up the drive, kitten hips swaying in the skin-tight hot pants.

Judd watched her progress. 'You must admit she's tasty,' he said.

'I don't care what she looks like,' Alyson retorted. 'Mike may have invited you, but he didn't invite her. Did he?' she faltered, abruptly unsure.

'No.'

With relief, she clambered back on to firm and righteous ground. 'In that case I can't sanction your turning this house into a—a bordello!'

'That's a bit strong,' he demurred.

'She's not staying here,' Alyson enunciated, through clenched teeth.

'But there's plenty of room in my bed, and you only need to look at her to know she doesn't eat much.'

'I don't give a damn if she exists on air, the only way she gains entry is by fighting me first!'

The doorbell rang.

'Then you'd better tell her,' said Judd.

Alyson looked at him. 'Me?'

'I've never set eyes on Miss Cutie-pie before.'

'You haven't? You mean she isn't——'

He grinned. ''Fraid not.'

Silence. Alyson cleared her throat, but when she next spoke her voice was croaky. 'I—um—seem to have—um——'

'Jumped to the wrong conclusion?' Judd finished. 'Entirely. In total. Made a complete hash.' The bell rang again. 'Time you answered that. What are you planning—a run and a dropkick, or is it to be a bare-knuckle event? Pity there's no mud for you to wrestle in. The sight of two sexy young women slithering around—mmm!' His eyes were rolled in theatrical glee. 'Like me to referee? Regrettably I don't have a copy of the Queensberry rules handy, but——'

Alyson gave him her brightest smile, the one she used on people she would love to slap silly. 'Shut up!' she snarled, and with head held high she stalked past him and out into the hall.

CHAPTER THREE

'GOOD afternoon,' said Alyson, as she opened the front door.

'I have come to see Gary,' the visitor announced, in an accented voice.

'I'm sorry, but Gary's in France and he won't be back for a month,' she explained.

'Ah,' the girl said, 'only he told me it would be OK to crash out here for a couple of days.'

'You're a friend of his?'

The flaxen head bobbed. 'We met when he was in Sweden last year.'

'Gary's parents, Mr and Mrs Brown, are also away,' Alyson told her, 'and I'm just here to look after the house. So I'm afraid that——'

'Excuse me, please, but what is your name?'

'Alyson——' she darted a look over her shoulder at Judd '—Fleming,' she said defiantly.

'I am called Anne-Marie Gustaffen and I come from Stockholm.' The girl held out a slender tanned hand. 'It is a pleasure to meet you.'

'Hello.'

'May I stay—just until Monday when I have a ticket for the ferry?' she requested, pouting appealingly.

Judd joined Alyson at the door. 'Sorry,' he said, 'but the property doesn't belong to us.'

'You are looking after it too?' Anne-Marie enquired, wide grey eyes flickering up and down him.

'No, I'm here as a guest. Mr Brown and I are friends.'

There was a dazzling, white-toothed smile and she held out her hand again. 'It is a great pleasure to meet you.'

'Hi,' he said.

'And your name is?'

'Judd Hamilton. As I said, we aren't the owners, so you'll understand we're not in a position to allow——'

'I don't suppose you can afford a hotel?' Alyson interrupted.

The visitor shook a regretful head. 'I've been hiking around England for a month and my money is almost spent.'

'Then we don't have much choice, do we, Judd?' Alyson enquired.

He frowned at her, frowned at Anne-Marie. 'Give us a minute,' he muttered, and drew Alyson back from the door. 'You can't intend to provide board and lodging?' he hissed.

'Why not? She seems well brought up and not the type who'd wreck the place, but in any case we'll be here.'

Although her immediate response had been to apologetically despatch the visitor, the advantages of having someone else around had dawned. Judd had always inspired her to extremes—when she had loved him it had been with every cell of her being, and when she had hated him it had been with equal zeal—and now, despite the determination to be coolly mature, Alyson was aware of feeling too wound up, excessively underpinned, altogether *agitated*. One look and she had decided a stray hitch-hiker was his lover! Wasn't that proof of an overheated mind? Regrettably, Judd had knocked her off balance, and it would be futile to deny that the prospect of staying here alone with him did not loom as an emotional hazard. However, if a third person was present to act as a buffer, albeit just over the weekend, her tension would have time to slacken and she could return to her normal safely tranquil frame of mind.

'A handshake and a few polite words means the kid's Goody Two-Shoes?' Judd protested. 'You're too trusting. Hell, she could be a sneak-thief, a confidence trickster, a drug trafficker!'

'Never!'

'Maybe not,' he allowed begrudgingly, 'but she's turned up out of nowhere, and you don't know the first thing about her, and this is the Browns' house, and——'

'And Gwen Brown would be most annoyed if we turned away one of her son's friends.'

'You reckon? How come you didn't give a toss about ejecting one of her husband's mates?' Judd demanded.

Alyson's chin lifted. 'That was different. You possess the funds to find alternative accommodation and you're not a young girl alone in a foreign country. We can't send her wandering off, not when the evening's approaching and it will soon be dark,' she protested. 'All kinds of dreadful things could happen to her.'

'She's been wandering for four weeks without coming to any harm, and although she might be young she looks a pretty tough number to me. My car's in the garage,' he continued, 'suppose I run her to the nearest station, give her a few quid, and——'

Alyson stepped forward. No matter what he suggested nor how reluctant he might be, Anne-Marie represented a saviour.

'Welcome,' she said, and as he stood frowning in the background she ushered the girl indoors.

Had she come far today? Alyson enquired, adopting the role of gracious hostess. No, just from a friend of a friend's near Oxford. Had she been to Sussex before? Never, but she hoped to visit some historical sites over the weekend.

'Try Battle,' Judd said drily, 'they have an abbey there.' All of a sudden, a volley of distant barks indicated that the dog had awakened. 'Would you like me to give him a run?' he enquired.

'Please. His lead's hung up alongside his basket, and Mrs Brown said if you turn left out of the drive there's a meadow roughly a quarter of a mile along which is free of sheep and cattle,' Alyson explained. 'You get into it over a stile.'

'Fine. See you later.'

'Is Judd your friend as well as Mr Brown's?' Anne-Marie questioned, as he strode off.

'We know each other from the past,' Alyson began, then stopped. The exertion of being cool and hysterical at the same time had been strenuous, and she felt suddenly drained—and in no mood to start explaining their relationship to a stranger who looked bright-eyed and distinctly interested. 'But that's all,' she completed.

The girl grinned. 'He's cute.'

'You think so? He likes the look of you too,' said Alyson, thinking this might make amends for Judd's unconcealed dissent and noticeable lack of welcome.

Anne-Marie's grin spread. 'He does?'

'Very much. Let me show you where you'll be sleeping,' said Alyson, and led the way up to a room where cream and navy-blue frills dominated, and which, like Judd's, was situated at the rear of the house. 'The bathroom's there,' she explained, gesturing across the hallway, 'and beside it is a separate shower-room. I must go and sort something out for dinner, but come down when you're ready. I'll be in the kitchen, it's through the door on the left at the foot of the stairs.'

An investigation of the freezer cabinet quickly revealed that Mrs Brown's determined quest for homemaking excellence incorporated food. No bags of shop-bought frozen chips or pizzas languished here. Instead there were home-made veal pomodoro, *poulet grand'mère*, stuffed fish turbans in oriental sauce and other exotic-sounding dishes, all neatly packaged, dated and labelled with cooking instructions. And, in a special 'desserts' section, mint syllabubs and cream gateaux were stacked, together with something called lemon flummery. Spoilt for choice, Alyson finally decided on apricot-baked bacon with duchesse potatoes and garden-grown broccoli, followed by orange, prune and apple ice-cream. Some microwave thawing was necessary, but soon the joint rested in the oven and the vegetables sat waiting.

'You enjoy to cook?' an accented voice enquired as she was in the midst of setting the table, and she looked up to see Anne-Marie.

'If I had enough time I would, but I don't, so I tend to live on ready-made meals and carry-outs. Mrs Brown prepared this evening's dinner and everything else you'll eat here,' Alyson told her, and explained about the freezer.

'Why do you not have enough time?' the girl queried.

'Because I run a business—which is how I come to be looking after the house,' she replied, and was required to give another explanation.

The facts she provided were clear and sufficient, but the visitor was not satisfied. Exhibiting a ravenous hunger for information, Anne-Marie proceeded to ask so many hows and whats and whys about Homeminders that Alyson, who was not usually averse to talking about her company, began to feel quite numb.

'It's a shame you've missed Gary,' she broke in, needing a diversion.

Anne-Marie tossed her head and the ruler-straight flaxen hair which had been resting on one smooth brown shoulder swung to lie on the other. 'It is of no importance.'

'But if it's a year since you've seen him——'

'Gary and I are not intimate,' the girl stated, and her head was tossed again, returning her hair to its original position.

Alyson watched in fascination. How did she do that? she wondered. And what was implied by 'intimate'? Anne-Marie's English might not be as fluent as it appeared and, contrary to common terminology, she could have used the word to mean something entirely innocent; yet hadn't there been a sexual nuance?

'Is Judd married?' the girl enquired.

'He was, but——' Alyson concentrated on arranging knives and forks '—not any more.'

'And you're not married either?' Anne-Marie demanded, gazing pointedly at her unringed fingers.

'No.'

'You prefer a career to a husband and a baby?'

Alyson felt the sharp stab of distress. What she would prefer was an end to the questions, *all* of them. 'For the moment,' she replied.

Whether the tightness in her tone was responsible or whether the girl lost interest, it was impossible to say, but the quizzing swerved.

'Is Judd involved with anyone?' Anne-Marie queried.

'No idea. You'll have to ask him,' Alyson replied, and, as if on cue, he walked in.

The breeze had fanned his dark hair across his brow and his skin glowed. With his tanned muscular arms and long legs, he looked supremely fit and athletic.

'Something smells good,' he grinned, appreciatively eyeing the meat which was browning behind the oven's glass door.

Anne-Marie stepped forward. 'Do you have a girlfriend?' she demanded.

'Nope. I'm fancy free and free for anything fancy,' Judd told her cheerfully. He bent to pat the Great Dane which stood, panting and docile, beside him. 'What's the routine for feeding this monster?' he asked Alyson.

'He has a meal around now, but Mrs Brown promised to leave instructions in the cupboard with his bowl.' She nodded towards the utility-room. 'Through there. Perhaps you could see to it?' she said, determined that, even though she was officially in charge, Judd would contribute his share to the running of the household. There might have been a time when she would have skittered around in circles single-handedly attempting to cater to everyone's needs, but those days were long gone.

'Will do,' he agreed. 'And when are we to be fed? After all the exercise and fresh country air, I'm starving!'

'Dinner will be ready in about an hour,' Alyson told him, 'so I thought we could have a drink first.'

'Good idea.'

'What would you like?' she asked Anne-Marie.

'Gin with tonic, please.'

'The same for you, Judd?' she enquired, remembering how it had been his choice in the past.

He shook his head. 'I'll have something soft. Cola, fruit juice, whatever's in the fridge.'

'We can use the Browns' booze so long as it's replaced,' Alyson told him.

'Maybe, but although I still have the occasional lager, I've cut out spirits. Not a drop has abused my liver for the past twelve months.'

Her hazel eyes stretched wide. 'You've stopped smoking *and* drinking?'

'A regular saint, aren't I?' The corner of Judd's mouth dimpled. 'Just about the only excitement I haven't banished from my life is sex.'

Alyson felt a traitorous pang. 'I didn't think you would,' she replied, and frowned at the dog. 'Rio also appears to be starving. Please would you give him his dinner now?'

With its Regency furniture and black marble fireplace, the drawing-room seemed too grand, so Alyson carried the drinks tray through to a smaller circular room which formed part of the original oast-house and which Mrs Brown had termed the 'snug'. Wood-panelled, maroon-carpeted and containing a curved chintz sofa which had been specially made to fit, this room also possessed an air of formality, but if anything did get spilled it shouldn't be too catastrophic—and when Judd reappeared Anne-

Marie showed far greater interest in capturing his attention than in noticing where she positioned her glass.

'Englishmen are much more stimulating than the Swedish variety,' the hitchhiker informed him, with what was beginning to seem a programmed toss of her head.

Judd drank a mouthful of spring water. 'You reckon?'

'I do.' She smiled at him along the length of the sofa. 'And I prefer older men.'

As if a switch had been flipped, he became wary. 'How old are you?' he asked.

'Eighteen.'

'You like Englishmen of, say, thirty-three?' Alyson asked from her chair opposite, and was rewarded by Judd's scowl.

She grinned blithely back. Acting as a third while he dallied had held no appeal, but if Anne-Marie wished to go a-wooing that was fine. It would reduce the pressure on her and—she glanced at his tight expression—also promised to be amusing.

The girl gave a fervent nod. 'They have so much to offer.'

'In what way?' she prompted.

'Conversationally, financially and sexually,' Anne-Marie replied.

Alyson almost choked on her orange juice. Although she had asked the question, she had never expected such a straight-from-the-shoulder answer. Was this a Scandinavian trait, or could she be listening to a generation gap? she wondered. Whichever, at eighteen she could never have spoken with such aplomb.

'What do you do for a living, Judd?' Anne-Marie continued.

'Right now, nothing,' he said briefly, as though whatever he said might be taken down in writing and used in evidence against him.

Alyson stared. 'Nothing?' she echoed.

'I'm unemployed. I gave up my job a fortnight ago,' he told her.

'But why?' she protested. 'You were so enthusiastic about being a dealer. You used to reckon that although seeing who could make the most money was risky, the excitement compensated a thousand times. You thrived on the lack of formality, that it wasn't a nine-to-five job, the satisfaction of seeing results immediately. You said it gave you a tremendous high.'

'It did.'

'So what changed?'

'Me. I grew older.' He flashed her an on/off smile. 'I hit thirty-three.'

Anne-Marie sat forward. 'I do not understand this word "dealer". Please could you explain?'

'Fundamentally, a dealer is a legalised gambler, though there are different kinds. Some work on the Stock Exchange, others, as I did, on the Foreign Exchange,' Judd explained, his wariness easing a notch now he was no longer being actively pursued, 'but whether it's shares or currency it's a matter of buying at one price and selling at another, and using your intuition to make a profit.

'You got out because you lost your confidence?' Alyson asked, recalling how he had once said that dealing was all a matter of nerve.

He shook his head. 'I woke up one morning and realised that if I continued to eat, drink and sleep dealing there was a grave danger of burn-out. But I don't want to self-destruct, I want there to be life after forty.' He took a slug of water. 'It was obvious that a lot of things needed to be re-evaluated, so I decided to stop, take time off to decide my future, and start all over again.'

'That's very brave,' Alyson remarked.

Judd's mouth took on a wry slant. 'Naturally I've done some saving, but even so when I remember there'll be no pay-cheque next month I break out in a cold sweat.'

'Have you decided your future?' Anne-Marie asked.

'Not yet. That's why I'm here, for a change of scene and to continue some serious thinking.'

'You have no idea what will come next?' she demanded.

'None. I've had a couple of offers from merchant banks, but for now I'm keeping my options open.'

'The offers were not lucrative?' the Swedish girl questioned.

'On the contrary, I'd be very well paid.'

'So why do you not accept?'

'Because money is not my main aim,' Judd replied, becoming irritated by this probing from someone who, an hour ago, had been a total stranger. He turned to Alyson. 'Most of the things I'd thought important now seem unimportant and vice versa, so I'm looking for something which will be satisfying but which will give me time to live and explore other interests.

'The banking jobs would not do that?' Anne-Marie enquired.

'No,' he said, the monosyllable sharp with impatience.

'But surely——'

'I intend to avoid executive stress, and so long as financial ends are kept within hailing distance I'll be happy.' Again he directed his words towards Alyson. 'A while ago a study was done of over two hundred dealers, and signs were found of high anxiety, psychosomatic complaints and coronary-prone behaviour patterns. Over ninety per cent were regular drinkers and it was discovered that dealers smoke more than the average white-collar worker.'

'Which is why you've eliminated spirits and the cigarettes?' she said.

'And why I'm now playing squash and swimming on a regular basis.'

'I saw a pool from my window,' Anne-Marie intervened, wafting an arm, and her glass, in the general direction. 'Perhaps we could have a midnight swim?'

'Not me,' said Alyson, apprehensively eyeing the swashing liquid. Did gin and tonic stain carpets, she wondered, and how about chintz? 'After working flat out until lunchtime and then driving down here, all I plan to be doing at midnight is sleeping.' Her mouth tweaked. 'But perhaps Judd will join you and even skinny-dip?'

She received a drop-dead look. 'No, thanks,' he replied. 'I'm having an early night too.'

Anne-Marie pouted and sipped her drink, but a moment later she revived. 'You said you play squash, Judd. Where do you play? In a private club, or——'

For the remainder of the evening, the hitch-hiker's curiosity continued unabated. Questions about sporting facilities moved into an avid interest in English social life, then became a cross-examination on the London entertainment scene, and on and on. At ten-thirty

Alyson decided she had had enough and, as she said goodnight, Judd professed acute weariness too. By eleven o'clock the oast-house—and Anne-Marie—were blessedly silent.

CHAPTER FOUR

'I'D BE obliged if you wouldn't encourage the Scandinavian *femme fatale*,' said Judd, as he came into the kitchen the next morning.

Alyson placed slices of wholemeal bread in the space-age toaster. 'In what way?' she enquired, all wide-eyed innocence.

'Lay off provoking an interest in me! You know very well what I'm talking about,' he rapped, 'but although you might consider it prime time comedy, I don't. She scares the hell out of me.'

'Not the pants off you?'

'This isn't a joke, I'm serious,' he grumbled. 'I told you not to let her in, and I was right.'

'You're being *too* serious,' Alyson protested. 'So she's a bit outspoken——'

'A bit!'

'—but that's just her way. She's young, and Swedes do have a reputation for being frank and forthright. All she wants is to get to know you—as a fellow member of the human race,' she recited, grinning, 'and perhaps enjoy a mild flirtation. After all, you did tell her you were fancy-free and free for——'

'I never imagined she'd fancy *me*,' Judd cut in.

'Why not? I did—once,' Alyson added, with pert emphasis.

'But I wasn't old enough to be your father.'

'You're barely old enough to be Anne-Marie's, though I don't see that age matters. Girls often date men twice their age, and——' she darted him a glance '—older women have been known to toy with boys.'

'Fair enough,' he replied, apparently deaf to any nuance, 'but I don't want to be seduced by a teenybopper!'

'You're over-reacting,' Alyson protested, 'and please could you unplug the coffee? Thanks. Anne-Marie isn't a *femme fatale* and she doesn't want to seduce you,' she said, as he placed the jug on the table. 'She indicated that she liked you, that's all.'

'Perhaps you're right.' He sighed. 'Perhaps I do have her pegged all wrong.'

'How about a deal?' Alyson suggested, as the toast popped up. 'I'll promise to be the soul of discretion, so long as you're nicer to her.'

'Nicer?' Judd enquired cautiously.

'I'm not asking you to grab her into a clinch. It's just that you could have been more welcoming yesterday. After all, she is a visitor to this country, and a guest.'

'Your guest, not mine,' he shot back, then he expelled another breath. 'A deal it is. I gather you didn't let on that we're divorced?' he continued.

'I didn't tell her anything about—about us.'

'And escaped a two-hour interrogation? Very wise,' he remarked pungently. 'Are you intending to make a start on your accounts today?'

Alyson nodded. 'What are your plans?' she enquired.

Judd went over to the window. 'I had meant to spend time by the pool, but it doesn't look as though there's going to be much sun,' he said, frowning out at a pale and hazy sky. 'I'll have breakfast, walk the dog and then decide.'

She put the toast rack on the table and sat down. 'How are your parents?' she asked.

He shot her a quick look. 'They're both fine, thanks. Is your mother keeping well?'

'Yes, though she can always find some ache or pain to grumble about.' Alyson made a face. 'Correction, she can always find something to grumble about, period.'

'You still trot along to see her every couple of days?'

'No.'

'No?' Judd echoed, in surprise.

'I go, but not as regularly.'

'The "I told you so's" got you down?' he enquired.

She nodded, unsettled by his perception. Although she had been publicly surprised, disappointed and awash with sympathy, her mother's private response to their divorce had been very different. Some thirty years after her own marriage had expired, she continued to regard herself as a deserted wife and a victim, and had taken a mean triumph in welcoming her daughter to the fold. She had always known their marriage would not last, Mrs Fleming had declared, but Alyson should be grateful she had not been left with a child to raise—like her. For a husband to go missing was cruel enough, but single parenthood was not a fate she would wish on anyone. On hearing this, Alyson had been beset by a tumult of emotions—disagreement, regret, fierce sorrow—and from then her visits had been kept to a minimum.

'Does your father still play golf most weekends?' she enquired, determinedly switching back to his family.

'Yes, and my mother continues to grieve over her favourite daughter-in-law's departure.' Judd's blue eyes hardened. 'Virtually every time we meet, she slides in a remark about how much she misses you.'

Alyson bowed her head. In contrast to her mother, her mother-in-law was a lively, warm-hearted woman and, as with Judd's brothers' wives, she had drawn her eagerly into the family. A bond had been formed between them which—maybe because she had been deprived of generously given female affection—had been close. This had made the failure of her marriage all the more distressing, for it had not only separated her from her husband, but also from a cherished friend.

Her throat tightened. 'I miss her too.'

'She says you should have kept in touch. I've explained that it's not that you don't want to see her, it's circumstances which—— I think I'll drive to the coast this morning,' Judd declared, in a swift change of tone and topic, and Alyson looked up to find Anne-Marie walking through the door.

'You are going sightseeing?' the new arrival enquired.

He shook his head. 'I thought I'd have a jog along a beach somewhere.

'A jog sounds fun,' came the pointed comment.

There was a long pause, during which Judd glanced at Alyson. 'Would you like to come with me?' he asked at last, in a voice more generally associated with 'bring out your dead'.

Anne-Marie beamed. 'Yes, thank you. And maybe,' she pleaded, 'we could see some sights afterwards?'

There was another pause.

'Why not?' he said.

Now committed, Judd went the whole hog and suggested a tour of the area which would include a visit to a castle and a pub lunch, and mid-morning he and his companion departed.

Alyson installed herself in the study and set to work. At one she broke off for a sandwich, but quickly resumed her labours. Engrossed in checking figures, sorting out invoices, trying to make sense of petty cash vouchers, she found time flew by. The crunch of Judd's Jaguar on the drive took her by surprise, and when she looked at her wristwatch she was amazed to discover it was almost five o'clock.

'How's it gone?' Judd enquired, coming in a few minutes later.

Alyson sat back. 'Wonderfully,' she said, with a contented smile. 'Have you had a good day too?'

He slumped down in an easy chair, one long leg thrust over the arm. 'No,' he said.

'You've been bombarded with questions?' she asked sympathetically.

'The questions I can cope with, it's the bombardment of advances that set me on edge.'

Alyson grinned. 'You're sure you're not overreacting again?'

'No way! You reckon Anne-Marie isn't a *femme fatale*, but how come the minute we arrive at the beach she strips off to an itsy-bitsy bikini and starts parading up and down before me? She's wearing the damn thing now. She's barrelling back and forth in the pool doing a hundred lengths,' he explained.

'Females do wear bikinis on beaches,' Alyson protested. 'I have been known to wear one myself.'

'I remember,' said Judd, and his gaze slid to her breasts. 'You fill yours much better.'

When his eyes lingered, she gave a hasty downwards glance. She flushed. That morning a loose filmy black shirt had been pulled on over a pair of tight white leggings, but as she had stretched across the desk two of the buttons had come undone, and the shirt had fallen open to reveal an alarming expanse of high smooth-skinned curves.

'If you're such an exercise freak how come you're not doing a hundred lengths with Anne-Marie?' Alyson demanded, hurriedly fastening.

'She suggested I join her, but——' he grimaced '—not this baby. As an excuse, I told her my eyes were sensitive to chlorine—and then she said I had beautiful eyes!' Judd burst out, in moral outrage.

Alyson also thought that his eyes, clear blue and fringed with long, impossibly curly black lashes, were beautiful, but she was not about to tell him.

'You're confusing the comments of a girl from a different culture with a deliberate come-on,' she said coolly, and began to clear away her papers. 'There's fillet steak in the freezer, so I thought we'd have it for dinner with jacket potatoes and a salad. Sound OK?'

Judd sighed. 'Sounds perfect.'

Now alerted, Alyson kept watch, but although admittedly the Swedish girl did make her crush a little *too* obvious, she could see no real reason for Judd to be so uptight. During the evening, there were adoring looks and the occasional 'come and get me' type comment, but that was all. Anne-Marie could well intensify her pursuit when she wasn't around, Alyson acknowledged as she climbed into bed, but a man of six foot two and in the peak of condition should be able to protect himself!

Some time in the middle of the night—was it?—Alyson's subconscious gradually absorbed an awareness of a warm body nestled close against her back and an arm hooked around her. The knowledge that it was a firm *male* body slowly infiltrated. With a contented murmur, she wriggled deeper into the bed and deeper into his embrace. Ever since her marriage, she had never enjoyed sleeping alone, and having a man beside her was bliss. She felt so cosy and protected. She felt at peace. Alyson was aware she was dreaming and she did not want the dream to end. Not now. Not ever. If only she could summon this fantasy every night, she thought hazily. If only she could conjure up the dream man to order. Drugged with sleep, she lay there wallowing in pleasure until, restlessly, she stirred. Lying like spoons, feeling his body against hers was impossibly sensual. She wanted the man to make love to her. Please. It was her dream, an inner voice reminded her, so she could make it happen. Alyson turned towards him.

'Sweetheart,' he sighed, as she snuggled closer.

Like a capsule coming from outer space and travelling nearer and nearer, growing larger and larger, being focused clearer and clearer, reality arrived. The man was not a dream. He lived, he breathed, he had spoken. Alyson jerked awake. The man was Judd!

Her head thudding with shock, she reached out and fumbled to switch on the concealed lighting around the pink velvet headboard.

'This might be a game to you, but I'm not playing,' she declared, sitting bolt upright.

'Mmm?'

'Would you please go!'

'What?'

She glared down. Judd's eyes were closed, his dark lashes spread on his cheeks, and he hadn't moved.

'Get out of here.' She prodded him. 'Right now!'

He yawned and ground big fists into his eyes. He had, it appeared, been fast asleep. 'Something the matter?' he muttered, squinting against the light.

'You! You can't creep into my bed!'

Blearily he gazed up at her. 'I wasn't...doing anything.

Reminded that, just moments ago, her one hope had been that he would 'do something', Alyson felt her cheeks begin to burn.

'You can't sleep with me. Go back to your own room,' she ordered.

'No. How long have you been coming to bed naked?' Judd enquired, his gaze suddenly sharpening.

She grabbed at the sheet and clasped it to her breasts. 'I forgot to bring a nightdress,' she said primly.

'You arrive with enough gear to last for six months and yet you neglect to pack something to sleep in?' he protested, yawning again. 'And I used to marvel at how organised you were!'

'You did?'

'Always.'

'I left in a rush. Are you wearing anything?' Alyson demanded, in sudden consternation.

The subdued light illuminated his bare chest where a smattering of dark hair outlined firm pectoral muscles, but now she tried desperately to remember whether or not the thighs and legs which had rubbed so intimately against hers had been naked. It seemed alarmingly likely, for Judd had always slept in the nude.

The corner of his mouth quirked. 'Would you like me to show you?'

'Er——'

It was too late, for, with a piratical flourish, he yanked back the sheet.

'Surprise, surprise!' he exclaimed, revealing maroon pyjama trousers.

Alyson knew a moment of relief. 'What do you mean, no?' she protested, abruptly realising she had been sidetracked. 'You must return to your room.'

'I can't, because if I do the chances are she'll come in again.'

She looked at him in surprise. 'Anne-Marie?'

'Who else? Minutes after I went to bed she appeared, panting to be ravished. I told her to go away—that I had a headache,' Judd said sarcastically, 'but half an hour later, what do you know, she slunk back again.' He pushed himself up on the pillow. 'Thanks to you.'

Alyson's brow puckered. 'Me?'

'Apparently she wasn't in the house ten seconds before you advised her that I was mad for her, which, in turn, prompted her to decide I was *made* for her.'

'Oh,' she said.

'That's what this whole thing has been about.'

'She actually came into your bedroom?' Alyson protested.

'And offered me a smörgasbörd of sexual delights? Amazing though it might seem, yes. You'd never be so brassnecked, but then you'd never need to be. All you need to do is look at a man with those big brown eyes and he comes running.' Judd's gaze dropped. 'And if you wandered in damn near naked, well——'

When he had thrust aside his portion of the sheet, her covering had, Alyson belatedly realised, been diminished, and she hurriedly readjusted the pink cotton in front of her.

'What did you say when Anne-Marie returned the second time?' she asked.

Judd sighed. 'I went through a long rigmarole about the two of us hardly knowing each other, and the days of the one-night stand being over, and how I wasn't interested in a Romeo and Juliet routine.'

'Then she disappeared?'

'Yes, but only to think about it! I should never have listened to you,' he carried on, his impatience gathering. 'A mild flirtation was all she wanted, you reckoned. Huh, her type of female doesn't know the meaning of mild! Females like her are dangerous. All it takes is for a fellow to give a few smiles and be neutrally pleasant, and they conclude he's interested. And if some clown happens to let it drop that he's dying of unrequited love—hell's teeth!'

'I didn't say that. I just said——' Alyson gave a shamefaced smile. 'I'm sorry.'

'I knew I recognised the gleam in Anne-Marie's eye and I know persuading that type of female they leave you cold is wellnigh impossible. I should have trusted my own judgement,' he declared, his voice thick with irritation. 'I should have remembered how blind you can be where other women are concerned.'

Alyson frowned. She had been blind in the past? When? Then she realised he must be referring to Sophia. Although that situation had been quite different, it was true she had not seen what was happening. Indeed, she might as well have been wearing a blindfold. Her thoughts were brought back to the present. All the signs that Anne-Marie was, as Judd had initially declared, a tough number—plus a seductress—had been there. It was evident in the way she dressed, in the coquettish toss of her head, in her statements—which had not been so much blunt as brazen. And while the hitchhiker might have claimed not to have been 'intimate' with Gary, she was obviously not averse to spreading her favours around—or trying to.

'You think Anne-Marie might approach you again?' she enquired.

'Alyson, I wouldn't be here if I didn't! I've checked the master bedroom, but, as with my room, the door doesn't lock, so there's nothing to stop her from bowling in.'

'But if you laid it on the line that she doesn't appeal?'

'I have! I've been as direct as possible without causing a scene, believe me, and I have no inclination to get into anything too heavy—shouting and maybe tears—in the middle of the night. Would you?' Judd demanded.

Alyson sighed. 'No.'

The previous year she had been required to dismiss a lover from her life and so had first-hand experience of the kind of tempest which could ensue. Then she had been pounded with arguments, pleas, enticements and—finally—accusations of hard-heartedness and mal-treatment. Never mind that they had both known she was right and he was very much in the wrong, sending him away had been neither pleasant nor easy.

'The only bedroom Anne-Marie won't come into is this one,' Judd said, 'which is why I came in. But I never planned to sleep with you. At first I sat on the edge of the bed, then I lay down and I zonked out. I guess my unconscious forgot we weren't married any more and that's how I ended up between the sheets. Suppose I kip down on the floor?' he suggested.

'You think you'll be able to sleep?'

'I can try.'

Alyson frowned. 'How long were you in bed with me?' Judd turned his wrist to scrutinise the black-faced watch which was strapped there. 'A couple of hours.'

'Two?' she echoed, in astonishment. 'But Anne-Marie must be dead to the world by now.'

'And if she's not? Or suppose she went back to my room a third time, found it empty, and decided to wait there in bed for me?'

'You think she would?'

'I think anything's possible,' Judd said wearily. 'Aly, I've already spent a good portion of the night here.'

She frowned. She supposed she was to blame for the girl hounding him—at least, in part.

'You might as well remain,' she said, though common sense warned she could be making a faulty decision. But it was the middle of the night, and, although an intelligent argument against him staying had to exist, her mind was too tired to construct it. 'I've brought a baggy T-shirt,' she said, sliding out of bed to scuttle across to a chest of drawers, 'so if I wear that and you lie on top of the sheet—but under the duvet—and I lie beneath, and we each keep to our own sides, and you promise to behave——'

'Me behave?' Judd protested. 'You think I'm lusting after you?'

'No, no.' The shirt was pulled hastily on and when her head emerged, her cheeks were pink and her blonde hair was tousled over her eyes. 'It's just that—um——' Alyson ran out of things to say.

'Have I ever pounced on you before?' he demanded. 'Have I ever raped you?'

'Of course not!'

'And I assure you, I'm not about to start now.' A smile bloomed in the corner of his mouth. 'Disappointed?'

'No!'

'Sure? You did turn and squeeze up closer.'

She avoided his eyes and his amusement. 'I was dreaming,' she declared, and climbed back into bed and switched off the light.

'Goodnight, sleep tight, mind the bugs don't bite,' chanted Judd, through the darkness.

'Goodnight,' Alyson answered stiffly.

She lay on her back. Rigid. It was a double bed with ample room and there was no reason why they should come into contact, but—— She did not want to move her legs and brush against his, even though the sheet was between them. She was wary of turning over and accidentally touching him. How could she have ever slept so peacefully and for so long with Judd close beside her? she wondered. How could she have been so unaware and yet felt so safe? How could she have longed for him to make love? Stretched out as stiff as a statue, Alyson listened to the steadying rhythm of his breathing. The trouble was, she wanted him to make love to her now. She knew she was only feeling this way because it had been a long time since she had been so close to a man—an undeniably sexy man. She knew it was only because Judd was familiar. She knew the love they had once shared had ceased. And yet she wanted him with an intensity that made her skin feel hot and tight, that made her heart pump, that made her *ache*.

'It's not just my mother who pines from time to time,' Judd said, all of a sudden.

Alyson jumped. She had been so sure he was asleep and now she felt caught out. It was as though he had looked into her mind and had seen what she was thinking.

'I—I beg your pardon?'

He rolled over to stretch his arm across her and spread a long-fingered hand on her waist. 'I've missed you too,' he said softly.

To know he had not simply wiped her from his memory, but that he still thought about her, seemed absurdly comforting, and a warm glow infused her. Turning her head, she smiled at him through the shadows.

'And I've missed you,' she said. Face to face in broad daylight she would have stayed quiet, but the dark was like a world apart and had made her brave.

'Much?' Judd whispered.

The days, weeks, months, years of feeling incomplete and restless clicked through her mind like so many woebegone film slides.

'Yes.'

'Oh, Aly,' he murmured huskily, and suddenly he was holding her tight and kissing her.

She knew she should protest, but, as his mouth opened on hers and she felt the eager probe of his tongue, Alyson abandoned herself to a giddy surge of elation. Winding her arms around his neck, she pushed her fingers into the thick dark hair which grew low at the nape of his neck. Its coarseness against her fingertips was as she remembered. His skin smelt the same too—clean, with a faint tang of lemon-scented cologne.

'I want you,' Judd muttered, his voice low and driven. 'I want to be inside you. I want to feel you all around me—moist and hot and tight.

He ripped the sheet from between them and swiftly dispensed with their clothes. Alyson quivered. A voice was yelling in her head, telling her that to give herself to him would be madness, but she had no choice. Their mutual nakedness was intoxicating, and in a sinuous movement she rubbed against him. Judd sighed, and, as though he was committing her body to his memory all over again, his hands began to move, cupping a breast, stroking the line of her slender waist, gliding across the thicket of golden curls that nestled between her thighs.

Alyson pressed closer, her body soft and yielding, her hands exploring and inciting him on, her mouth a fevered temptress. With a groan, Judd grasped her buttocks and steered her against his thighs, and as she felt his hardness the blood that ran in her veins became electrified quicksilver. His hands claimed her breasts, his fingers plucking at the taut straining tips until she gasped out loud. This was the rapture she had craved, she thought, as she writhed against him. This was the passion. He lowered his head and his mouth covered her nipples, and as he licked hard with his tongue and suckled, Alyson gasped again.

'Sweetheart, I'm sorry, but I can't——' Judd muttered, and twisted her beneath him.

He might have made love nonchalantly once, but now a frenzy of need had consumed him. Now his breath came in harsh rasps and as he entered her his thrust was urgent. Alyson's hips began to gyrate and heat flooded her body. She felt so tender, so ready, so open.

With an incoherent murmur he pushed deeper, his tempo quickening. Reasoned thought vanished, now all Alyson knew was the delicious agony of sensation. Her head began to spin, and she was coiling, looping, circling, flying. Together they rocked, passion equalling passion, until in one marvellous moment the world seemed to explode—and suddenly she was falling, falling, convulsed by the throes of satisfaction.

* * *

Alyson was on the brink of falling asleep again, when a thought suddenly hit—like a fist between the eyes.

'Oh, no!' she exclaimed. 'You could have made me pregnant!'

'You aren't using any kind of birth control?' Judd asked drowsily.

She reached out and switched on the light. 'None. Why should I? I don't usually—I never thought that tonight we'd——' Her voice trailed away. She had known she was making the wrong decision in letting him stay. She had known they should never have made love. Damn it. Damn him. Damn her own stupid needs. 'I don't suppose you've been sterilised?' she enquired hopefully.

'No!'

'Then what am I going to do?' she wailed.

Judd yawned. 'Don't worry, nothing'll happen. Not after just one time.'

'It could. It did when——' She stopped short. 'It is possible,' she insisted.

'A one-in-a-thousand chance.'

'But suppose that chance comes up?'

He gave an impatient sigh. 'Being pregnant isn't a fate worse than death.'

'You wouldn't want to be a father,' Alyson retorted. 'You hated the idea when we were married.'

Judd frowned. 'No, I didn't.'

'You did! Maybe initially you were agreeable, but later—— '

'Alyson, if we'd had a child,' he said heavily, 'it might well have kept our marriage intact.'

'What!' In outrage, she stared at him, the blood pounding in her temples. 'You're rewriting history,' she declared, and stretched over and yanked the sheet from him. 'I don't care if Anne-Marie is still on the prowl. You're not staying here a minute longer!'

'But——'

'Go!'

Judd sighed, then held up his hands in weary surrender. 'No need to shriek. I hope you sleep well too,' he said sardonically, and climbed out of bed and disappeared.

Alyson doused the light. How dared he make out he would not have minded a child! she thought furiously, but moments later her indignation collapsed. And why did he have to say that one would have kept them together? She tried to block out the memories, but it was no use. Her mind melancholy, she stared into the darkness and, once again, began to relive the past . . .

CHAPTER FIVE

A thriving laundry service which specialises in the provision of quick-speed shirts requires energetic young manager/ess to take charge of an area between the Embankment and London Bridge. The chosen person will have full responsibility for their own territory. In addition to generous basic salary a volume-related commission will be paid, so this is a great opportunity to— *etcetera*.

ALYSON had been flicking through the 'situations vacant' column in a cursory fashion. Although her job as a secretary with a firm of building contractors had become humdrum of late she was not actively seeking a change, but phrases which included 'Take charge of your own destiny' and 'Why vegetate in an office all day?' caught her eye. When a letter had arrived asking her to attend for an interview she'd felt mildly pleased, but by the time the interview had ended she was brimming with enthusiasm.

'Many City brokers have neither the time nor the inclination to do their own washing and ironing, and, in any case, will only wear a properly laundered shirt,' Sophia Carter, the firm's managing director and owner, had explained, 'so my twenty-four-hour desk-to-desk service is extremely popular. I've always believed image to be important and, as well as being intelligent, any girl I employ must be well-groomed and pretty. She'll wear a specially designed navy pin-striped jacket and skirt, and have a brand new company car, plus mobile telephone.'

The job sounded impressive, but Alyson was even more impressed with Sophia. The interview had taken place in her stylish black and white office which was located on an élite Mayfair street, and throughout it the brunette had deftly juggled telephone calls, solved problems for various members of her staff, scrawled an exotically looped signature on a sheaf of letters. Alyson had never met a woman so accomplished, so sure of herself, so vivid. Beautifully dressed, bone-thin, and with so many ringleted curls they could knock you sideways, Sophia gave the impression of being in glorious Technicolor while everyone else was in black and white. Gazing in awe, Alyson had wondered whether when she reached the forty-ish stage she would be so efficient and so chic. It seemed doubtful.

When she was offered the job, she felt flattered to know she had met Sophia's standards. Now her days were spent acknowledging the orders which bleeped on her portable phone, collecting and delivering shirts around a multitude of offices, and, in between times, dispensing leaflets to attract new customers. The number of shirts her area generated, and her commission, were beginning to grow when she had met Judd.

One look across a room of flickering computer screens, one laundry order given, and both were captivated. Six months later they were married. Sophia, who claimed the role of matchmaker, professed herself delighted, and her relationship with Alyson, which had been strictly employer and employee, underwent a change. Alyson presumed that now she was married the older woman regarded them more as equals, and so felt inspired to draw her—and Judd—into her social circle.

'Trevor spends weeks away on business, but he's home at the moment, so I thought I'd give a dinner party for a few chums,' her boss had said, a month or two after they had returned from their honeymoon. 'We'd be delighted if you and your husband would join us.'

Once again Alyson had been impressed, for Sophia's home, a duplex apartment in Chelsea which overlooked the Thames, was spacious, pale-hued, and classy. The meal had class, too. Where time had been found to prepare the iced soup, the veal in cream sauce, the enormous raspberry pavlovas which fed the sixteen guests who comprised the 'few chums', she could not imagine. Her own workload was heavy, yet Sophia's was heavier. Hadn't she spoken of problems which constantly demanded her presence at the laundry? Hadn't she talked about interminable meetings with equipment suppliers? Hadn't she sighed over the tedious lunches she was forced to endure persuading chairmen and company chiefs to allow her staff access to their employees?

'What do you think of Sophia?' Alyson had asked, as she and Judd had driven home that night. He had never met the woman and now she was eager to have his opinion.

He made a face. 'Engaging, but brittle.'

'Brittle?' she had protested.

'I know she has you well and truly hypnotised, yet although she's charming, vivacious, *etcetera*, underneath it all is one tense lady.'

Initially Alyson had rejected his criticism, but a few days later she had witnessed two incidents which indicated that he could be right. First, Sophia rounded on her secretary, who was still pale and weak from the 'flu, and accused her of malingering, and, second, she issued a vitriolic rebuke over a forgotten order and reduced another of her manageresses to tears. Alyson accepted the validity of Sophia's demands that her employees should work hard—she never coasted, so why should they?

—but she could not agree with her acting the tyrant. For the first time, the thought that her idol might possess flaws sneaked into her mind; until a conversation had explained everything.

'Do you and Judd have plans for children?' Sophia enquired, as Alyson came to the end of yet another weekly report of increased orders.

'Not immediate ones. We want to spend time getting to know each other before we start a family,' she replied, and smiled. 'So I'll be with you for another couple of years.'

'Don't take a family for granted,' the older woman warned. 'Trevor and I have been trying to have a baby for ages, but this far—no joy.'

The revelation came as a surprise. Alyson had blithely believed that, as it had said in the advertisement, Sophia had charge of her own destiny, and thus had assumed it was from choice that children did not feature in her high-gloss life. But now she understood why she had been so sharp-tempered, and forgave her. In a similar situation, she knew she would have been exceedingly edgy.

'After all kinds of tests, the doctors insist there's nothing physically wrong with either of us and there's no reason why it shouldn't happen,' Sophia went on, 'but Trevor's so often away he doesn't allow me a proper chance to conceive, and time's running out.' She had given a laugh which *was* brittle. 'If I'm ever going to have a child, what I need is a man who's always around and always eager. You're lucky,' she continued, 'Judd's home every night, even if he does work long hours.'

I'm lucky *because* he works long hours, Alyson had thought secretly. As a brand new wife, she had regretted her husband leaving home around seven in the morning and not returning until twelve hours later—at least, because business entertaining sometimes kept Judd out all evening—but she had soon realised that if there were to be decent meals and if she was to keep on top of the washing and the cleaning, her solitary hours were essential. On finishing work, she dashed around the shops and, once home, flew straight into action.

To begin with Judd had helped with the chores, but this had been short-lived. In all honesty, Alyson had not minded too much, for he had been so lackadaisical it had quickly become apparent that if she wanted anything done properly—and she liked their home to be spick and span for when friends and relations called—the only way was to do it herself. But she had never realised how much slog housework involved. Whatever she did and no matter how hard she tried, her efforts seemed to be simply a process of containment. Had their weekends been free, her weekdays need not have been so hectic, but Judd said—and she agreed—that as they both worked hard, they deserved to play hard, and Saturdays and

Sundays were a carousel of visiting and being visited, of trips to the theatre, the cinema, restaurants. Alyson enjoyed it all, and yet, despite her wanting to be vibrant and good company, there were times when she simply felt exhausted.

When she had hinted at this, Judd had suggested they employ a daily help, but she had refused. Sophia managed on her own—marvellously—and so would she. Sometimes, however, Alyson did wonder whether she had her priorities straight. Medals were not awarded for best washed windows, and Judd ate his meals so quickly she was sure he barely tasted them. For the most part, he also seemed insensitive to her efforts in their home. His work, of course, absorbed many of his thoughts as much as his time, but she wished he wouldn't just stroll blindly and casually around, leaving clothes everywhere for *her* to pick up. Still, she was a new wife and, she assured herself, once she had more experience everything would fall into place and be much less trouble.

Over the next twelve months, the volume of shirts Alyson handled multiplied. In the main, she was pleased. With Judd doing so well in his career, it was good to know that, in her own field, she was a success—and she loved the pride he showed in her. But dashing around all day meant that by evening her energy was depleted, and somehow getting a proper grip on the housework invariably eluded her. Indeed, she still had the feeling of needing to run, simply to keep up. So—one year on, there was no reduction in her activity and, one year on, she and Judd had become regular guests at her boss's home.

As much as she liked Sophia, Alyson also liked her husband, who had a very different personality. A short, solid-looking man, Trevor was bluff and down-to-earth. They got on well together. His firm grasp on reality also appealed to Judd, and the two men had hit it off from the start. With regard to Judd and Sophia, he might have called her 'brittle', but he had also said 'engaging', and if, at times, he made ironic observations about what he considered to be her craving for the limelight and her love of glitz, their relationship was friendly. Indeed, the older woman became decidedly skittish whenever he was around. She was also interested in his job as a dealer.

'Judd, you're a man who knows about money,' Sophia said one evening, as Trevor went off to organise after-dinner liqueurs. She flashed a smile at Alyson, who was talking to another guest, and drew him towards the balcony. 'Could I have a word?'

'What did Sophia want to speak to you about?' Alyson had enquired that night, when they were getting ready for bed.

Judd undid his tie and tossed it on to a chair. 'Just needed a spot of financial information,' he said, and ambled away.

But a couple of months later, when Sophia and Trevor came to dine with them, the older woman had again engineered a private chat. A second time Alyson had enquired as to its content and a second time had received a vague reply—which, on this occasion, had made her feel uneasy. Once she and Judd had shared everything, but suddenly it struck her that they were sharing less and less. One reason was shortage of time—some weeks the pressures of work and play allowed no opportunity to sit down and *talk*—yet when they did their conversation showed an increasing tendency to dry up. Why? Unhappy with the feeling that they might be growing apart, Alyson resolved to pursue the subject of his chat with Sophia—until Judd had returned, tumbled her on to the bed, and given her other, infinitely more exciting things to think about.

Another month on, Alyson's head was spinning with just one thought—that she might be pregnant. She had forgotten to take the Pill, they had made love once but at an apparently crucial time, and now it appeared their plans to wait had been wrecked. Initially, she had felt wrecked too. To have a child when her job was going so well and while they were living in central London was lousy timing. It would strap her in and cramp their style. However, Alyson had decided she did not mind. Looked at from the bright side, her pregnancy would enable her to give up her frenzied life, and that held an undeniable appeal.

But how would Judd react? He would be surprised and maybe even shocked, yet once he got used to the idea she felt sure he would be delighted. However, it seemed politic to break the probability to him gently.

'About a baby,' Alyson began, as he poured himself a pre-dinner drink one evening.

Instantly his shoulders stiffened and he swung round to frown at her. 'What about it?' he demanded.

'I—well, I wondered how you felt about us having one sooner rather than later?' she faltered, unprepared for such a brusque response.

'No, thanks.'

'We did say we'd have one next year.'

'We said we'd *start* one next year,' Judd corrected.

Alyson gave a coaxing smile. 'But next year is only six months away.'

'At which time we'll review the situation.'

Her smile faded. A baby had been debunked, dismissed; it no longer featured on his agenda? She felt a tremor of dismay. An appointment had yet to be made with the doctor and so her pregnancy was not a cast-iron certain, but all the signs pointed that way.

'You've—you've changed your mind?' she queried.

Judd took a swift mouthful of gin and tonic. 'I just think we shouldn't rush things. There's plenty of time.'

'But we agreed!'

He shrugged. 'Now we disagree.'

It had been a trying week. Because on Monday he had informed her that he would be working late each evening, Alyson had decided to have a blitz on the curtains. Every pair had been either hauled to the dry-cleaners or washed, but some of the washed ones had refused to iron satisfactorily and a couple of lengthy hems had come undone and needed to be re-sewn. After much frustration the curtains were back in place—though Judd had not so much as glanced their way!—and now her mind felt the strain.

'We don't disagree, you do!' Alyson flared.

It was unusual for her to lose her temper, and a horror of becoming like her mother meant she rarely complained, but his casual dismissal had been too much.

Judd came to sit beside her. 'Don't get upset,' he appealed.

'What else do you intend to disagree about?' she demanded.

'Nothing.'

Alyson dashed away the hand he had placed on her knee. 'How do I know that? And while we're on the subject, I want to put it on the record that I'm strongly opposed to being left on my own night after night after night. It would be a treat if, just occasionally, you could pencil me in for dinner!'

Judd frowned down into his glass. 'I'm sorry about the late nights, I don't like them either,' he said, and sighed. 'But they are necessary.'

His sigh sounded so weary and dejected that her anger collapsed. If she had been without him, equally he had been without her. He had not deserted her from choice, but because his work demanded it—and life on the trading floor was no rest cure.

'Is something bothering you?' Alyson asked, suddenly aware of lines of strain around his eyes.

Judd gulped from his glass. 'Not a thing,' he replied, and got to his feet. 'There are some phone calls I need to make and then we'll eat. All right?'

Everything had *not* been all right, but Alyson had recognised she was getting ahead of herself and that, before she raised the subject of a baby again, her pregnancy must be confirmed.

As anticipated, the result was positive, but now all she had felt was apprehension. Perhaps, when he was handed a *fait accompli*, Judd's attitude would change? Perhaps he would decide he wanted to be a father immediately? Perhaps he would be thrilled? But he had been surprisingly antagonistic, so perhaps not? Perhaps he would accuse her of forgetting to take the Pill on purpose?

Faced with these imponderables, Alyson had felt a need to talk the matter through. What she required was an older woman who would listen as she verbalised her thoughts and, perhaps, provide reassurance. By tradition her mother should have filled the role, but she invariably hijacked conversations and substituted sharp-tongued recitals of what she regarded as her woes. Judd's mother would have been ideal, except that she *was* Judd's mother. So who else could she approach? The only other immediately accessible older woman she knew was Sophia. Although wary about discussing the problem of her pregnancy with someone who so much longed to be pregnant herself, Alyson decided to risk it. Sophia was a poised woman of the world, but if she should detect any reluctance or signs of distress, she could always stop.

After completing her orders the next morning Alyson drove to the Mayfair office, only to discover that her employer had gone out.

'She's lunching with some man at that snooty French seafood restaurant in Knightsbridge,' Sophia's secretary, a gamine redhead with a penchant for dangling earrings, informed her. 'She didn't give me his name, but whoever it is he must be special, because she's gone to have her hair done first. She reckoned it was a business meeting, but if you believe that you'll believe anything.'

'Excuse me?'

'Not too particular about keeping to the straight and narrow is Madam Sophia.' The redhead's tone was sneering. Ever since the 'malingering' episode, she had been un-enamoured of her boss and never missed an opportunity to criticise. 'You're one of her "chums", you must have realised how partial she is to the opposite sex.'

Alyson's brow furrowed. Had she realised? Now that she thought about it, she supposed she had. At her parties, Sophia made a beeline for the men and spent most of her time laughing and chatting with one or another.

'Madam isn't happy unless she has at least a couple of males paying court, preferably younger ones,' the girl went on. Her voice lowered into sly confidentiality. 'Rumour has it that every time Trevor goes away she dons her glad-rags and sidles out to meet——'

'What time do you think Mrs Carter will be back?' Alyson enquired. Sophia was a good employer and a generous hostess, and she had no wish to listen to malicious gossip.

The redhead's mouth pinched. 'Her lunches can last for ever, but she's usually through by three.'

Wary of another wasted journey, Alyson checked with the office at half past three, but Sophia had not returned. At four she was still absent. And at five. Now all available time had gone, but the following evening the Carters were holding another of their soirées, so she decided to wait and attempt a tête-à-tête then.

Sophia never sent invitations sparingly, she despatched them in bulk, and when they arrived at the riverside apartment they found it thronged with architects, barristers, businessmen and their wives—a crowd whom Judd had mockingly termed 'the beautiful people'. One of Sophia's rules was that everyone must circulate, which meant she was always swooping on couples and splitting them up, and after the buffet supper Alyson found herself talking to a trio of virtual strangers, while Judd was nowhere in sight. It had happened before. She was looking for him when, through the crowd, she suddenly saw her hostess going out to top up drinks. With an excuse to her companions, Alyson followed. All evening she had been looking for an opportunity, and a quick chat in the kitchen would be ideal. At least, she tried to follow, but a middle-aged lawyer who had been persistently ogling her stepped in front as she neared the door, and it was a few minutes before she managed to extricate herself.

As Alyson walked down the corridor, the murmur of voices wafted out from behind the almost closed door. Sophia was not alone, she had a man with her—though it could not be Trevor, because he was in the living-room. Alyson sighed. Her talk was private and confidential, she would need to come back later. Foiled again. Curses! She was turning to retrace her steps when she heard her hostess give a sudden ringing laugh of delight.

'Oh, Judd, sweetie,' Sophia exclaimed, 'I knew you'd be the one to help me. I just knew!'

Judd had left the party and was closeted away with Sophia? Alyson did not know why, but she felt a sudden flicker of calamity.

'In error,' he grated.

'Was it?'

'Yes!'

'Whether or not, what does it matter?' Sophia said lightly. 'All that matters is——'

'It *does* matter,' Judd insisted, 'and I don't consider I have helped you. No way. If I'd known what it was going to lead to——'

'You'd have never agreed,' his companion completed for him.

'You can stake your life on it!'

She laughed. 'Sorry, sweetie, but it's too late now.'

There was a pause.

'You must realise you're playing a dangerous game?' he demanded, in a troubled voice.

'Don't worry about it. OK, Trevor must never know what's happened, or rather how it's happened, but—oh, Judd, I'm so happy, and it's all thanks to you. The future looked bleak, but now—— Oh, Judd,' the brunette exclaimed again, 'whatever would I have done without you?'

Alyson's brows knitted. She knew she ought not to eavesdrop, but what were they talking about? What assistance could Judd have performed, albeit by mistake?

'The future won't be plain sailing, anything but,' Judd said behind the door. 'You'll need to be careful.'

'*We'll* need to be careful,' Sophia corrected. 'You mustn't give our little secret away either, and especially not to Alyson. She'd be demoralised if she ever realised her beloved wasn't the shining example of perfection she imagines. I know you wouldn't tell her deliberately,' she said, when he began to protest, 'but confidences do have a nasty habit of slipping out in weak moments—especially if you have doubts.'

'I do have doubts. Severe ones,' he rasped. 'However, when I said to be careful I wasn't talking about giving anything away. I was referring to making certain that from now on—— What do you think you're doing?'

What *was* Sophia doing? With no help from her, Alyson's feet walked forward and she peered through the gap in the door. Her heart jack-knifed in her chest. Her hand clutched at the front of her honey-coloured catsuit. Judd and the older woman were locked in an embrace. He had his back to her, but the brunette's braceleted arms were wrapped tight around him—and when she drew back her smile was wide and satisfied.

'Thanking you and showing you how much I care,' she crooned. 'Don't panic, sweetie,' she said, as Judd raised a hand and began furiously scrubbing lipstick from his mouth. 'Trevor's in the middle of yet another of his dreary oilman's stories, so he won't disturb us.' She neatened the pillarbox-red bullfighter jacket that nipped her waist and smoothed her slim black skirt. 'I know you care for me too.'

'Sophia——' he started to protest, but scarlet-taloned fingers were laid across his lips.

'Don't deny it, you're wasting your breath. You'd never have come to my aid unless——'

'Are we expected to die of thirst?' a voice enquired, in jocular complaint.

Sophia clammed up. Alyson spun round. Two of the guests had grown tired of waiting for their drinks and were coming in search along the corridor. As they approached, Alyson shot the men a tepid smile and sped back towards the living-room. On the threshold, she halted. She could not rejoin the party. She could not make small talk. Not now. Impossible. She needed to be alone. She desperately needed time to *think*. The stairs were on her left, so she ran up them and turned the key in the glass door which opened on to a tiny and rarely used veranda. Her head pounding, she gazed down at the moon-silvered waters of the Thames.

In what way had Judd come to Sophia's aid? How could a woman whom she had believed to be her friend sneak away and kiss *her* husband? And why had Judd stood there and let it happen? Frantically, Alyson chewed at a fingernail. Her secretary reckoned Sophia had a weakness for younger men, so could she have been naïve? She had never noticed any special intimacy between them, but it had not occurred to her to look. Her heart fluttered. Her boss might be ten years older, but she was a charismatic woman and it would be easy to understand if she had bewitched Judd.

Placing her hands to her fiery cheeks, Alyson shook her head. No. No. No! Judd was not bewitched. There was an innocent explanation for what she had seen. Sophia had a tendency to gush, and the kiss had simply been an over-effusive gesture of thanks. Hadn't it? Yes. It had been a one-off, and was unimportant and nothing to be troubled about. As for the baffling conversation, when she spoke to Judd he would explain that too.

The pad of running footsteps sounded on the stairs and Alyson swivelled to see a tall, dark outline through the frosted glass. She smiled. Judd had come looking for her.

'What are you doing here?' he asked, as he stepped on to the veranda.

'Getting some fresh air—and some quiet.'

'Do you want to go home?' he suggested. 'Tonight's gathering is noisier than usual.'

'I wouldn't mind, but——' Alyson looked at her watch '—isn't it too early?'

'A bit,' Judd acknowledged. 'Tell you what, I'll have a smoke and then we'll make some excuse and leave. OK?'

She grinned. 'OK.'

Opening a packet of cigarettes, he placed one between his lips, then took a book of matches from his jacket pocket. As moonlight glinted on the metallic lettering, Alyson automatically read the name which was printed across the back. The matches had come from Le Quai Pompadour. It was the snooty French seafood restaurant in Knightsbridge.

'You had lunch with Sophia yesterday?' she asked, her voice teetering on a narrow line between disbelief and accusation.

Judd struck a match and the flame flared, lighting the planes of his jaw and his full mouth. 'As a matter of fact, I did.'

He was the 'special' man the secretary had talked about? He was the reason Sophia had failed to return to her office? Alyson could not have felt more betrayed if he had stuck a stiletto between her ribs.

'You never told me!' she protested.

'It was supposed to be a secret,' he replied.

'You and Sophia have *two* little secrets?' she demanded.

Judd inhaled, the tip of his cigarette burning red. 'I have no idea what you mean.'

'Like hell!'

He glanced over the rail to the balcony below and to the side, where other guests were gathered.

'Don't shout,' he said.

'I'm not shouting, I'm speaking distinctly,' Alyson retorted, her enunciation diamond-hard. 'For a start, I mean the pair of you have just been kissing in the kitchen.'

Judd frowned. 'You saw that?'

'And I heard.'

'What did you hear?'

'Enough to know something is going on,' she declared.

'Not so loud!' he protested.

'*Has* been going on, perhaps for a very long time,' Alyson went on, in a fierce hiss.

'You're talking nonsense!'

'Then would you please explain your secret lunch—and all those absent evenings when you were supposedly at the office being the dealing *wunderkind* and making vast amounts of cash for your company.'

The latter remark had been thrown in wildly and without reason, but now she watched in horror as Judd's face took on a cornered look. The evenings had significance.

'I also know I'm being made a fool of,' Alyson continued, suddenly perilously close to tears, 'and that maybe——' she took a breath, flung back her head and glared '—maybe we should be thinking in terms of a divorce.'

Judd cast a frowning look over the veranda. 'Maybe,' he murmured.

The ground seemed to fall away from under her, and she needed to clutch at the rail in order to remain upright. Although she had never acted the tragedienne before, tonight—perhaps because pregnancy was playing havoc with her hormones—Alyson had felt a need for high drama. Yet she had not truly believed 'something was going on', nor did she intend them to separate. All she had wanted was a thundering row in which Judd would answer her charges and clear the air, followed by a long and passionate reunion. But instead everything had blown up in her face!

Alyson gazed at the darkly moving river. She was well aware that marriage came with no guarantee label, and she knew Judd was more laid back about it than she—more laid back about everything—but when he had vowed to love only her 'until death us do part' she had believed him. She had trusted him. She had never—ever—imagined he might stray. OK, he had claimed her talk of a long-time affair was nonsense, but that did not exclude a fleeting one. Indeed, why would he accept the idea of a divorce unless he had been unfaithful? Unfaithful when they had been man and wife for eighteen short months? her mind protested. Unfaithful when she was just a few weeks pregnant?

Invisible hands seemed to claw at her throat and suddenly it was difficult to breathe. At the start of the evening she had believed their marriage was strong and inviolate, yet now it seemed to be in an advanced state of decomposition. She glowered at Judd. He had cheated on her. He had defrauded her. He had trampled over their love.

Alyson swallowed hard. But maybe she should be more laid back herself? Affairs were nothing new. Hadn't she read somewhere that almost half of all married people cheated on their partners at some time or another? Her thoughts went to how edgy Judd had seemed recently, and how his consumption of cigarettes had increased until now he was almost chain-smoking. His involvement with Sophia must have been troubling him—certainly, he had sounded irritated with her in the kitchen.

Did that mean he regretted their affair and it was doomed? She swallowed again. If so, then maybe she should forget about it and pretend it had never happened. Could she do that?

All of a sudden, there was a movement on the landing and someone pushed wide the door.

'I wondered where you two were,' Sophia said, and imperiously clapped her hands. 'Inside, quick, quick! I have an important announcement to make.'

Beside her, Alyson was aware of Judd stiffening.

'Do you know what this is about?' she demanded, as they obediently followed their hostess down the stairs.

He shook his head. 'No idea.'

Sophia waited until everyone had gathered in the living-room and then, when silence had fallen and she had positioned herself centre stage, she began to speak.

'Trevor and I wanted to share our news with our oldest and dearest friends and tell them that at long last our dreams have come true, and——' a bejewelled hand moved in a prima donna flourish '—I'm pregnant!'

As cheers rose up all around and glasses were held high, Alyson was beset by a series of flashbulb memories. She remembered how she and Judd sat in silence, where previously the conversation had flowed. She saw Sophia complaining about Trevor's being away so often he never gave her a chance to conceive—and now Judd was available every night. She heard again the talk in the kitchen of how she would be demoralised. Pow!—something snapped in her head. Judd, it appeared, was the father of Sophia's baby.

In one breath she felt stupefied, angry, isolated and panic-stricken. Now she knew how he had spent those absent evenings. Now it was clear why he had been against her having a child. Faced with a pregnant mistress, he would not welcome a pregnant wife! But what was going to happen to her and, more particularly, to her baby? Alyson wondered in confusion. To be born into a family with a loving father was everyone's birthright, and Sophia's child would have Trevor, but Judd did not want the embryo that nestled in her womb. He did not seem to want their marriage either. She blinked back tears. Although it was fashionable to discount the importance of a father in childhood, she knew what it was like to be deprived. How many times had she yearned for a father to look after her, to lift her on to his shoulders, to boast about—like the other children? Undoubtedly Judd would help on the financial side, but what about the essential aspect of the baby's life—its emotional welfare? Was it to be brought up hardly knowing him? Must it be doomed to missing out? Was its childhood to be unhappy?

Alyson had solved the problem in the only way she knew how, though it was a way destined to haunt her waking and dreaming hours. And when, a few months later, Judd had suggested they go their separate ways, she had agreed.

CHAPTER SIX

HIS elbows on the table and sections of one of the weightier Sunday newspapers spread around him, Judd was catching up on world events.

'Congratulations,' he said, as Alyson came into the kitchen. 'I was wondering whether you'd make it down by midday, and you have—with ten minutes to spare.'

'Everyone's allowed a lie-in,' she demurred.

'I agree.' His blue eyes fixed on hers like heat-seeking missiles. 'Especially when their sleep's been disturbed by erotic congress.'

'Was Anne-Marie lying in wait when you returned to your room?' she enquired, refusing to respond.

'No, and she didn't drop in later either. I was left to slumber in peace—praise be. Let's hope that when she puts in an appearance today she'll leave me in peace again,' he said drily. He closed up the newspaper. 'Aly,' he began, his face becoming grave, 'with regard to last night——'

'You enjoyed the erotic congress? So did I,' she said, being gloriously flippant. 'It's a long time since I've had a fling.'

'A fling?' Judd repeated.

'What else would you call it? Is the coffee hot?'

'Should be.'

'How about the toast?'

'That's fresh too,' he said impatiently. 'I've not been up very long myself.' He frowned. 'For you, last night was just a—— It didn't mean anything?'

'Like what?' Alyson asked, pinning on a smile of bright enquiry.

Judd hesitated. 'Well...we were once married.'

She poured herself a cup of coffee and reached for the milk. 'What difference does that make?'

'Well——' he said again, but this time it was as far as he got. He pushed back his chair. 'I'll take Rio for a walk,' he muttered.

When he had gone, Alyson heaved a sigh of relief. She had decided that the only way to deal with—and to negate—their chokingly sweet lovemaking was to be cool, calm and casual, and she had managed it. Last night had shown that some residual desire, and some residual liking, existed between them, but there it ended. Must end. Her sexuality might have turned traitor, but she had no intention of becoming further entangled. After all the traumas, her life was now on an even keel and Judd would not be allowed to disrupt it again.

Alyson had taken over the paper and was reading the news, when Anne-Marie wandered in a quarter of an hour later.

'I'm sorry I overslept. I hope I am not a nuisance,' the teenager smiled.

'As far as sleeping late goes—no. As far as marching into other people's bedrooms in the middle of the night is concerned—yes,' she replied.

Grey eyes rounded into surprised circles. 'You heard me?'

'I did,' Alyson declared, preferring a little inaccuracy to the truth, which would provoke reams of searching questions, 'and unless you agree to stop pestering Judd you'll have to leave.'

'Leave?' the girl echoed.

'This morning.'

Another decision Alyson had made was to solve the Anne-Marie problem. Her pursuit must be stopped—dead. After all, the last thing she wanted was Judd using her bedroom as a bolthole again!

'But I like him,' the teenager said sulkily.

'That's no reason to throw yourself at him. It's not only embarrassing for the poor man, it also makes you look silly. Have you no pride?'

There was a pout. 'You think I ought to play harder to get?'

'I think you should accept that Judd isn't interested and won't be falling for you, come what may,' said Alyson. 'He has made his feelings abundantly plain.'

Anne-Marie considered this. 'I suppose so,' she sighed.

'Then leave him alone!'

'I will.' More sighing followed, but it was not long before the girl smiled. 'In future, I shall be aloof and mysterious with men,' she decided.

'Sounds an excellent idea,' Alyson agreed.

'So may I stay until tomorrow?'

She grinned. 'Please do. Coffee?'

'Thank you.'

Showing amiable acceptance of the reprimand, Anne-Marie ate her breakfast. Afterwards, she helped clear the table and wash up, and subsequently asked for permission to swim. When Judd returned, she was streaking up and down in an energetic crawl.

'It's scorching hot and a perfect day to enjoy the pool,' he said, gazing out at where the sun shone on the terracotta tiles of the terrace and sparkled in the water beyond, 'but I'm damned if I'm going to go out there with her.'

'You won't have any problems,' said Alyson. 'I've told her to stop bothering you.'

He spun round. 'You've done what?' he demanded.

'I said to stop the sexual harassment. And if Anne-Marie should change her mind, she knows she'll be——' she jerked a thumb '—out of the door. I'm sorry if you think I was interfering,' she went on, when Judd continued to stare, 'but it seemed to me that as I was responsible for her taking a shine to you in the first place, it was up to me to——'

'I'm grateful you've warned her off—very,' he interrupted. 'What amazes me is you speaking out. Three, four, five years ago, you wouldn't have confronted her.'

'Never,' Alyson agreed, 'but I'm older and wiser now.'

'And tougher,' Judd commented. He grinned. 'So today I can lie alone by the pool with the Nordic maiden and be assured my chastity will remain intact?'

'You can, though you won't be alone, because I shall be lying out there too. I've fed the gerbils and lined up something for dinner, so——' She shrugged.

'How about you having another session with your accounts?' he suggested.

'They'll keep. Judd, it's Sunday and el collapso time,' she protested.

She *was* wiser, Alyson thought, as she went upstairs to change. In days gone by she would have worked regardless, but now not only were non-essential and time-wasting chores eliminated from her life, she also paced herself. It made for a lot less pressure and far more contentment. As for being tougher; although she did not consider she had been short of basic courage in the past, she had lacked confidence. This could have been due to immaturity—or maybe it was linked to growing up with her mother's unceasing negativism?—whichever, instead of attempting to take control of events, she had allowed them to control her. It had been a big mistake. However, since she had been on her own she had developed a new kind of strength, and now conflict did not scare her and she was prepared to hustle, if necessary.

Not much later Alyson found herself wondering if, by joining Judd at the poolside, she had made another mistake. Wearing brief black swimming trunks which hugged his thighs, he was altogether too muscular and too virile for her peace of mind. How could she ignore his smooth tanned flesh? How could she be blind to the grace of a body that tapered from broad shoulders to narrow hips? How could she remain immune to the masculinity which seemed to be coming at her in waves? Last night, he had awakened a need which had lain dormant for three years, for, alarmingly, it had not been a need simply for lovemaking, but an acute need for *him*. Why this should have happened, she did not know, and she certainly had no wish to analyse it.

'You aren't reading?' she asked, perching stiffly on the lounger he had set out beside him. 'You're just going to doze?'

He grimaced at Anne-Marie who was still doing lengths and stretched his arms in negligent ease. 'For now, yes. It may have taken me thirty-odd years, but I'm discovering that there are occasions when I like sloth. It's restful. Isn't it?' he said, talking to the dog which had begun to follow him around and was lying flat out alongside. 'I used to be far too work-orientated,' Judd continued. 'It was that old cliché, the yuppie syndrome. I wanted things quickly and I wanted them all at the same time.'

Yes, you wanted a wife *and* a mistress, Alyson thought.

She lay down on her stomach and opened the colour supplement. Her chin in her hand, she was busy reading when a fingertip touched the bone at the base of her neck and began to trace a leisurely line down her spine. Instantly, her skin tingled, her pulses raced, an ache flowered in the pit of her stomach.

'I can remember licking my way along here,' Judd murmured. 'It was most exhilarating. I like licking you. I like the taste of——'

She rolled over and sat up. 'You must have a very good memory, because I don't,' she declared.

A brow twitched, making it plain he was not reading her lips but her mind. 'No?' he said, and with cool deliberation his eyes began to roam her body.

As his gaze stroked over the fullness of her breasts and the curve of her hips, Alyson's heart started to pound. She had considered her mint-green bikini to be respectable—and compared to Anne-Marie's silver lamé contraption, it was—yet beneath his cool appraisal it shrivelled to wanton proportions. Unfortunately her body was beginning to respond in a decidedly wanton way too. Her skin felt itchy. Her nipples were pinching. The ache in her stomach had escalated into gnawing desire. Joining him out here *had* been a mistake.

'Do you recall the morning when I was shaving and you wandered into the bathroom half asleep?' Judd queried. 'You put your arms around my waist and proceeded to rub yourself slowly against me, and——'

'Please may I use this hammock?' Anne-Marie yelled, from inside the garden shed.

'—and very soon the silk of your skin replaced the silk of your nightdress on my back and shaving foam ended up in all manner of unexpected places.'

'Go ahead. Judd'll help,' Alyson called, desperate to end his reminiscences.

She did not need to be reminded of the passion they had shared—either in the past or last night. Indeed, making love with him loomed so large in her mind it was all she could do to keep still. So much for being cool, calm and casual!

'Now you *are* interfering,' Judd said tersely, but he pushed himself upright and walked over, accompanied by the dog.

In the shed, where more loungers, pool gear and all manner of gardening tools were stored, the Swedish girl had, it transpired, been searching for an inflatable mattress, but had come across an elaborately fringed double hammock instead. At the far end of the pool and on the edge of the lawn were two appropriately placed oak trees, and she thought it would be fun to swing between them. She was sorry to disturb him, Anne-Marie said, with uncharacteristic meekness, but fixing it would not take long.

Her assertion proved to be incorrect. Ten minutes on found Judd hot, glistening with sweat and becoming increasingly annoyed, and it was a further ten before the hammock was finally in place.

'If she'd taken the damn thing out in the same way it had been put in everything would have been fine,' he complained, marching back. 'Instead she drops it, gathers it up every which way, and gets the ropes hopelessly tangled. Sorting them out took ages, then she doesn't tie it tight enough to the tree!'

'The hammock looked as though it would have stayed up,' Alyson protested.

'For how long?' He dropped down on to his lounger. 'If you're going to do a job, do it properly!'

'So saith the man who, on the few occasions when he dusted, always dusted around and never under,' she murmured.

'You know why it was a few occasions?' Judd demanded, his irritation switching to her. 'Because you were so bloody particular. And it stands to reason that if I'd had more practice at housework I would have improved.'

'You'd have become a whizz in an apron and pink rubber gloves?' Alyson scoffed.

'I'd have given it my best shot, but whenever I participated you weren't happy. Maybe you never actually complained,' he said, rebuffing her protests, 'but it didn't take me long to realise that whatever I did on the domestic front you frequently did again—only better—so I thought, what the hell?'

Alyson frowned. There had been occasions when, in her eagerness for their flat to be immaculate, she had re-cleaned, but she had believed herself to have been discreet.

'And that's why you stopped helping,' she said, in a wondering voice.

'What was the point in two of us doing the same damn thing?' Judd scowled at Anne-

Marie. 'She's dripping all over the place,' he grumbled.

After a few swings in the hammock, the teenager had grown bored. Deciding that her personal stereo would liven things up, she had set off for the house and on the way had dived into the pool, swum across and climbed out again. Her subsequent dab with a towel had been brief and now, as she crossed the flower-tubbed terrace, she was leaving a trail of splashes and watery footprints behind her.

'Aren't *you* being too particular?' Alyson enquired, but Judd's criticisms continued.

'I don't know why she bothers to wear the top of her bikini,' he said scornfully. 'She's about as voluptuous as an ironing board—the same as Sophia.'

Alyson turned a page of the colour supplement. 'You used to like Sophia,' she said, keeping her voice painstakingly level.

'Not as much as you did. Close the door, otherwise the dog'll get in!' he shouted, but he was too late—Anne-Marie had disappeared and Rio was already climbing to his feet.

His expression stormy, Judd also rose. Given the chance, the Great Dane would, Mrs Brown had warned, scratch at cupboards and ruin paintwork, and so must not be allowed indoors alone. Muttering beneath his breath, Judd strode past the animal, but, as if sensing his mission, it increased its pace too. Judd put on an extra spurt—and so did his companion. Alyson was grinning at the neck-and-neck chase towards the house when, all of a sudden, Judd skidded on the wet tiles and his feet went from under him. With an agonised shout, he fell on top of the dog and, in a flurry of windmilling arms and furry limbs, the two of them crashed to the ground. A second later, pained yelps filled the air.

Alyson leapt up, but before she could reach them the Great Dane managed to struggle free.

'I do hope he's all right,' she said, as the animal shot past her like an express train and vanished into the orchard. 'You don't think you might have——'

Judd struggled into a sitting position. 'Forget the damn dog and worry about me,' he instructed.

'You?' she queried, for he appeared to be all in one piece, if somewhat red-faced, tousled and bad-tempered. 'Why, is something wrong?'

'My ankle. Don't touch it!' he squealed, when she bent to investigate. 'It's broken.'

'Can you move your toes? And your foot?' Gingerly, and with many pained grimaces, he did both. 'You've twisted it, that's all,' Alyson decided.

'All?' Judd protested. 'It hurts like fury!'

'There's a hospital a few miles from here, so I could drive you and their casualty department could check it over,' she suggested, when he continued to sit there and wince.

'Please.' He held out a hand. 'Can you help me?'

Disturbingly aware of how little each of them was wearing, Alyson helped him upright and provided a human crutch as he hopped slowly into the kitchen.

'I'll go and get dressed,' she said, when Judd was settled on a chair, 'and I'll bring you some clothes. What would you like?'

'Any shirt and a pair of shorts. There are some black ones on top of my case.'

As Alyson went upstairs, she met Anne-Marie coming down and so, without apportioning any blame, she told her what had happened. Instructions were given to restrict the dog to the garden, and, some ten minutes later, she and her still wincing charge departed.

Sunday afternoons appeared to be a quiet time for accidents, and Judd was rapidly examined and a verdict given. An internal ligament had been torn, though not badly, and he had what constituted a light sprain. All it required was for him to keep off the limb for a few days, and the ankle would quickly mend.

'I was intending to go back to London at the end of the week. Will I be able to drive?' he enquired.

'Sorry, I can't say. Make an appointment for Friday morning,' the doctor instructed, 'and I'll be able to tell you then.'

A supportive bandage was applied, a pair of crutches temporarily provided, and Judd hopped back to the car. For the remainder of the day, he was in obvious pain and subdued. The Great Dane, too, was quiet, though plainly it had suffered no broken bones either. Now, however, it steered well clear of Judd.

Although she regretted his accident, it did have one pertinent advantage, Alyson thought, as she settled down to sleep that night. It kept him in his room and out of hers. Anne-Marie might no longer threaten, yet he could have been tempted to visit her again. The stroke of his finger along her spine and the sensual memories he had insisted on reviving indicated as much. And if Judd came to her room, how did she keep him from her bed when all he needed to do was simply *look* at her and she throbbed with longing? Alyson sighed. The straight answer was—she couldn't.

The next morning Anne-Marie explained that in order to catch the ferry she needed to be on a bus which left the nearest town at one, and so must ring for a taxi.

'Don't bother, I'll run you in,' said Alyson. 'Rio's appointment at the kennels is for one-thirty, so I can drop you off and then deliver him to his destination. While he's being groomed, I'll do some shopping. I should be back around three,' she said, turning to Judd. 'Will you be all right on your own?'

'I'll be fine. Already my ankle feels much better. I can make my own lunch,' he said, when she suggested leaving him something. 'I may have been reduced to hopping, but I can still feed myself.'

On her departure, Anne-Marie bade Judd a short and demure goodbye, but when Alyson deposited her at the depot her farewell switched to fulsome thanks. With the Great Dane occupying most of the back seat, Alyson drove on. Mrs Brown had assured her that Rio loved cars and would be no trouble and, although she had been apprehensive, that was the way it turned out. He also relished being groomed, and when they reached the kennels he bounded in. Free now, Alyson parked at a black and white timbered shopping mall and enjoyed a leisurely stroll around. She finished up in a supermarket where, among other things, she bought herself an apple and a tub of yoghurt, which she ate as a snack lunch in the car. When she returned to collect the dog, his nails had been clipped and his coat was freshly shampooed and shiny.

It was minutes after three when Alyson arrived back at the oast-house. As the dog disappeared into his basket for a snooze—apparently being groomed was a tiring business—

she put away her purchases, then walked out on to the terrace.

'I thought you were here to think, not sleep,' she teased, finding Judd stretched out and yawning on a lounger.

'I've had a catnap, that's all,' he grinned. 'Are you coming to join me?'

Alyson dithered. Before going out that morning she had spent two hours on her accounts, and the intention had been to carry on. But. The day was warm and sunny, the sky above was blue, butterflies flitted from flower to flower—and the prospect of working away indoors held no appeal. If she was to take advantage of the good weather and the facilities which were currently being offered, shouldn't she do so now? The high temperatures might not last, and even if the sight of Judd in his swimming trunks continued to disturb her, he was mostly immobile and thus represented no danger.

'I'll go and change,' she decided.

Alyson had reached the top of the stairs and was turning towards her room, when she suddenly saw that the door of the master bedroom was ajar. She halted. Before going out she had shut all the doors as a fire precaution and a matter of standard practice, so why was it open now? Could the catch have slipped? Had the door—somehow—blown open? Intent on closure, she walked along the landing, but as she reached the doorway she halted again. A mirrored panel in one of the fitted wardrobes had been slid aside. Her brow creased. An integral part of Homeminders' arrival procedure was to check through the house to confirm that everything was in order, and she knew that when she had made her inspection the wardrobe had been closed. There was no way the panel could have moved on its own, so who had moved it and why? Crossing the wistaria-coloured carpet, Alyson peered inside. A long rail held a dozen or more men's business suits in dark colours, and as she looked at them her hand flew to her throat in horror. The sleeves hung in ribbons, there were gaping holes in the trousers, patches of cloth littered the wardrobe floor. With urgent fingers, she riffled through. Every single suit had been slashed!

In anticipation of more damage, she swivelled, her gaze travelling fearfully around the room, but the only other immediate sign of disturbance was a heavy silver photograph frame lying face-down on a bedside table. Alyson went to pick it up. Lying loose beneath the frame was the photograph it had once contained. The photograph had been torn in two, and when she pushed the halves together she saw it was a studio portrait of a man she recognised as Mike Brown.

All of a sudden, Alyson became aware of a strongly scented aroma and, sniffing, she followed it into the en-suite bathroom. Her hazel eyes opened wide. In the washbasin was a pile of pre-shave, aftershave and eau-de-cologne bottles, all opened, upended and drained, while on the marble surround and glass shelves stood deodorant sticks, shaving brushes and an assortment of other male toiletry items—each one cut and despoiled. Stunned, she stood there for a moment, then she turned and ran down the stairs and out to the pool.

'So much for you looking after House Beautiful!' Alyson declared, as she reached Judd. 'While you were happily snoring that man in a balaclava crept past you!'

Raising a hand to shade his eyes, he peered up at her. 'What are you talking about?'

'Someone's broken in.'

'There's been a burglary?' he said, in astonishment.

'Yes!'

Swinging his legs from the lounger, Judd sat up. 'What's been taken?' he asked.

'No idea. All I know is that clothes and various other items in the Browns' bedroom have been damaged, with a razor, by the look of it.'

'Aly, no one went past me, they couldn't have done. I only nodded off for five minutes, dammit!' he protested. 'I know because I checked my watch at three and you appeared not much later.'

'Well, someone got in somehow. Homeminders are supposed to protect homes!' wailed Alyson, as her blaze of anger burned itself out and anxiety took over. 'A three-hour absence is allowed, but suppose the Browns cut up rough and take me to court? Suppose it gets into the newspapers? Suppose——'

'Hold on,' Judd ordered. 'Gwen Brown fixed for the dog to be groomed today, right?'

'Right.'

'Then you not being here is her responsibility. Mind you, Mike's opinion of me is going to hit rock bottom when he discovers a burglary happened in my presence.' Reaching for his crutches, he heaved himself upright. 'I'll come and look,' he said.

In the master bedroom, Judd gave a low whistle of disbelief as Alyson showed him first the slashed suits and then the destruction in the bathroom.

'You didn't see any sign of a break-in at the front of the house?' he enquired.

'I didn't notice anything when I came in,' she said, 'but I'll go and check.'

'When you're downstairs see if any more items have been damaged and whether anything appears to be missing,' he instructed, 'and while you're doing that I'll take a look around the other bedrooms.'

Alyson sped off, coming back in due course to report that all doors and windows at the front and sides of the property were intact. 'And at the back—I checked there too,' she said. 'I can't find anything damaged downstairs and nothing appears to have been stolen either. What about up here?'

'Same tale as yours, no sign of any other disturbance.'

'Odd,' she said, frowning.

'Very,' Judd agreed. 'Why should whoever did this restrict themselves to just the one room?'

'Maybe the intruder suddenly realised you were beside the pool and decided it was too risky to stay any longer?' she suggested, wishing he would put on some clothes. Judd out of doors half-dressed had been bad enough, yet to have him hopping around the house in nothing but his trunks was incredibly distracting.

'But there are no signs to indicate that there *was* an intruder,' he said. The crutches were repositioned beneath his arms. 'You don't think Anne-Marie might be responsible? I admit it's a long shot,' he added, as Alyson stared at him, 'but suppose she wanted to get back at me for rejecting her?'

'And at me because I read the Riot Act?' She shook her head. 'I don't see it. I mean, why ruin the Browns' belongings and not ours? But she showed no sign of resentment when I warned her off, and even if she did feel a bit miffed she wasn't the type who'd seek revenge. Definitely not.'

'You're right,' Judd agreed. He indicated the bank of mirrored wardrobes on the opposite wall. 'Have you checked those?'

'Not yet. The suits and the chaos in the bathroom were such a shock, I didn't get any further.'

'You just hurtled downstairs and started tearing strips off me,' he said pithily.

She hung her head. 'I apologise. It was a knee-jerk reaction.'

'Apology accepted.'

Alyson grinned. 'Thanks. I'll start here,' she said, moving a panel aside, 'and go through everything.'

Judd swung himself over to a chest of drawers. 'I'll help.'

'Be thankful for small mercies,' she sighed, a minute or so later. 'None of Mrs Brown's dresses have been touched.'

'But Mike won't be wearing these shirts again,' Judd said, showing her a drawer full of tattered garments.

Further investigations revealed that while almost everything which belonged to Mr Brown had been mutilated, his wife's possessions were unscathed.

'Odder and odder,' said Alyson. 'You're sure you didn't hear any noises? Even though no one appears to have forced an entry, they could——'

'I did hear a noise,' he interrupted.

'Now you remember!'

'Don't get excited,' Judd warned. 'Some time after I'd had my lunch—it'd be around two—I heard footsteps on the drive. I was out by the pool, so I hopped around intending to ask whoever it was what they wanted. A woman had called, but by the time I reached the front of the house she was leaving and all I caught was a glimpse of her hurrying on to the lane. Seconds later, I saw her drive away in her car. She was a short dumpy type, wearing a blue two-piece and sensible shoes.' He shrugged. 'My guess is she was a neighbour.'

Alyson frowned. A few minutes ago an idea had sneaked into the back of her mind, but now it marched to the front.

'Did this neighbour have tightly permed greying hair and spectacles?' she enquired.

'That's right.'

'What kind of a car does Mike Brown drive?'

'A white Rover—and,' Judd said slowly, 'it was a white Rover that drove away.' He looked at her. 'You think it was Mike's wife who did a hatchet job?'

'Don't you? If he did attempt to sort out their problems but got nowhere, and then started talking about a divorce, she might have felt . . . aggrieved.'

'Aggrieved to the point of driving the three or however many hours from Warwick and sneaking in here to go berserk with a razor?' he protested. He rubbed a finger back and forth across his lower lip, a habit when he was thinking. 'And yet it fits. Her knowing you wouldn't be here and—presumably—not being aware of my presence, and only Mike's possessions taking a battering.'

'Plus the battering being a neat battering. If an outsider had been responsible they'd have strewn the clothes around, but the bedroom's tidy.'

'And Gwen Brown is fastidious.' Judd's fists clenched around his crutches. 'How could she be so vindictive? I've heard about hell having no fury like a woman scorned, but—strewth!'

'If there was talk of a divorce then obviously it would upset her, and maybe she felt a need to vent her hurt and this is her way of doing it?' Alyson suggested.

'The bitch!'

'Distress can drive people into all kinds of malicious actions.'

'You're trying to excuse her,' Judd protested.

'I'm explaining how Mrs Brown may have felt,' she replied. 'And don't forget that even now she could be regretting what she's done. Regretting it deeply.'

'Fat chance!'

'It's possible.'

'I assume you have the number of the hotel where the Browns are staying? I'd like it, please,' Judd instructed. 'Mike needs to be told what's happened.'

Alyson shook her head. 'No.'

'He damn well does!'

'Look, if Mrs Brown goes back to Warwick that will show she hasn't written off their relationship, not entirely—yes?' He gave a curt nod. 'But if you ring Mike and forewarn him he'll be furious, and the moment his wife walks in he'll pounce and all hell will break loose. And that'll reduce the likelihood of him forgiving her. However, if he isn't told and she's sorry and she confesses, then although he'll be mad perhaps he'll understand and they'll be able to smooth things over. Please, Judd, give Gwen Brown a chance,' Alyson appealed.

'She doesn't deserve one.'

'Why not? Everyone regrets something they've done. Everyone hits out at times.'

'When our marriage went sour you didn't hit out,' he said impatiently. 'You could have involved us in an expensive court case, you could have claimed a sizeable chunk of my earnings, you could have accused me of all kinds of faults——' he frowned '—but you didn't. You simply walked away. You didn't retaliate.'

'You're wrong. I did, and in a way which was far worse than destroying a few suits.'

'What do you mean?' Judd asked.

Alyson moistened lips which had suddenly gone dry. 'I mean,' she said, 'that I destroyed a baby.'

CHAPTER SEVEN

JUDD looked bemused. 'A baby?' he repeated.

'I forgot to take the Pill and I became pregnant and—and I had an abortion,' Alyson told him. 'And although there were a number of reasons, one of them was a backlash—against you.'

'You mean you discovered you were pregnant after we'd split up?'

'No, it was while we were still married.'

Stunned incredulity filled his eyes. 'What?' he protested.

'I started to tell you but, if you remember, you said you'd changed your mind about us having a family. At that stage the pregnancy had yet to be confirmed, so——'

His jaw clenched. 'If you intend to say I "hated" the idea of a child and I'm responsible for you getting rid of it, don't!' he grated, his confusion hardening into anger. 'I admit I wouldn't have welcomed one at that time, but I'm damned if I'll take the rap for——'

'I'm not blaming you,' Alyson assured him hastily.

'So—when did this abortion take place?' he demanded.

'Do you remember Sophia's party, the one when she announced that she was going to have a baby?'

'The night you gave me the first indication that our marriage might be over?' he said, a chilling edge to his voice. 'I'll never forget it.'

'The operation was a few days later. Afterwards I took the week off work and—and pretended I had food poisoning,' she said chokily.

Although Alyson had never foreseen an occasion arising where she would tell him what had happened, she had imagined how such a scene might be. In the belief that the trauma had been resolved and was firmly behind her, she had visualised herself as being calm and dry-eyed, but to her dismay she felt anguished and surprisingly weepy. It was as though the abortion had happened yesterday and she was still raw and bleeding.

'And I never suspected a thing!' Judd rasped.

'There wasn't much to suspect,' she replied, uncertain whether he was castigating himself for not having been sufficiently sensitive, or her for deceiving him. 'The pregnancy was in the very early stages—I hadn't really begun to think of the baby as a baby—so the abortion was performed under a local anaesthetic and virtually the only physical discomfort I suffered was a few stomach cramps.'

'Well done!' he bit out. 'But why did you feel a need to lash back at me?'

'Because——' she gulped down a breath '—because I thought the child Sophia was carrying was your child.'

Judd put his hands to his head as though to keep it from falling apart. 'For heaven's sake, surely you knew me well enough to know——'

'I jumped to the wrong conclusion,' Alyson mumbled.

'Something which appears to be a habit,' he said, with savage precision.

'I beg your pardon?'

'You jumped to the wrong conclusion when you first saw Anne-Marie.'

'Oh ... yes. I realise the affair with Sophia was brief and of no consequence,' she went on, 'and I know now you'd have made certain she wouldn't become pregnant. You never entirely trusted her, did you? However, at the time——'

'You realise what?' Judd broke in. 'I was *not* involved with Sophia, not sexually. I told you, dammit!'

Alyson frowned. 'I know, but——'

'But you didn't believe me,' he completed, in a leaden voice. His blue eyes looked straight into hers. 'I swear on all that's sacred that I did not go to bed with the damn woman.'

'No?' she said weakly.

'Never!' He picked up the threads. 'Sophia said she was pregnant and you thought I was to blame, and——?'

'And the morning after the party I tried to find out more about your relationship and discover what had been happening,' she said unsteadily. 'But when I asked all you would say was that it was "nothing special", and then——' Alyson made an ineffectual gesture '—you rushed off to work.'

'So you promptly rushed off and casually eliminated our child, *my* child?'

Tears stung at the back of her eyes. 'Judd, it may have happened quickly, but it was not casual.'

Her protest went ignored.

'Even though you had this cockeyed notion about me indulging in extra-marital relations, did it never occur to you that *I* ought to have been consulted?' he demanded, all muscle and glare. 'Did you never think that fathers should be allowed to state their opinions too? Did it never strike you that what you were doing could be described as unholy?'

'Not everyone would agree with you on the last point, but yes!' she cried. 'What I'd done literally laid me out flat for a week and worried me sick for months. It worries me now.'

Judd's fingers tightened on his crutches, their knuckles whitening as though he was fighting an urge to strike her.

'So it damn well should!' he denounced.

Alyson flinched. When she had imagined the confessional scene, she had never visualised that she would touch off such a tinderbox of resentment and anger. She had never anticipated this howling, gnashing protest. She had never thought Judd would care so much.

'Terminating that baby was the most regrettable and least excusable act of my life,' she continued. 'However, no matter how much I rue the day nor how full of remorse and self-reproach I am, it can't be changed. And it did happen more than three years ago,' she added, stretching out her hands, their palms open in supplication.

'But it happened!' He stabbed a finger. '*You* made it happen. It was *your* choice.'

'A choice which seemed valid at the time,' she protested.

'It was a bad choice.'

Alyson sighed. 'You may not have noticed, but there are a lot of them about. I believed our marriage was in jeopardy, and I felt vulnerable and alone. I was frightened. I saw history repeating itself, and the baby being me and perhaps me turning into my mother, and—and all kinds of other disasters, and I panicked.'

'You're nothing like your mother,' snapped Judd.

'No, and I accept that most of my fears were spectres manufactured by my imagination, but at the time they seemed *real*. Don't condemn me,' she entreated. 'I wasn't the first scared girl to have an abortion and I won't be the last. And after all, millions of women regularly expel embryos each month by using the "morning after" pill or the coil.'

'It was no big deal, is that what you're telling me?' Judd enquired, in a voice as cold as ice.

'No!' Her hair had tumbled over her eyes and Alyson pushed it aside in agitation. 'What I'm saying is that, whether or not you consider abortion to be an option of the emancipated woman or killing by another name, what I did is over and there's nothing to be gained from——'

'You cold-bloodedly disposed of my child!' he thundered.

'It was not cold-blooded. I went through agony before and afterwards I mourned. Deeply.' She looked at him, hoping for some small sign of compassion, but his face was grim and the set of his mouth uncompromising. 'Even if you can't forgive me, can't you at least try to understand?' Alyson implored.

'I understand why you're so keen to defend Gwen Brown,' Judd said bitingly, 'and I also understand why you knew the age of the Carters' son.' A nerve jumped in his temple. 'If you'd allowed our child the gift of life, by now he or she would have been——'

Alyson clamped her hands over her ears, she could not take any more. Tears blurring her vision, she turned and stumbled out along the landing and into her own room. Her shoulders heaving in a shuddering sob, she threw herself on the bed and began to cry.

That night her rest was fitful. Although her tears had fallen hard and long, they failed to sluice away the memories of the past. But now her memories had taken on a different slant, because now she knew Judd had been faithful.

After her long hours of nocturnal thinking, when she awoke the next morning Alyson felt weary and heavy-headed. Should she go back to London? she wondered, as she pulled on a buttermilk-coloured blouse and short fawn skirt. The idea was appealing. Yesterday, when her sobs had finally quietened, Judd had been out by the pool and so she had gone into the study—and spent the remainder of the day working first on the accounts and later on her tax return. On the few occasions when they had come into contact, her accuser's manner had been frosty and his exchange of words minimal.

Pensively she drew the brush through her hair. Leaving would mean an end to the friction and that would be a relief, but if she departed who would walk the dog between now and Friday? His damaged ankle had rendered Judd incapable. Yet did exercising rate as essential? The garden was large and provided ample room for the animal to wander. Matt bronze shadow was fingertipped on to her eyelids and her lashes were darkened with mascara. Another benefit to going might be that, if she tackled her tax return in normal work surroundings, the questions which yesterday had proved so difficult would—with luck—be easier to answer. Alyson frowned at her reflection in the mirror. But why should *she* be the one to retreat? It was Judd who had ranted and raved and insisted on treating her as the enemy, and if her presence offended him so much why didn't *he* remove himself from her orbit? There was nothing to stop him. He might not be able to drive, but he could always take a taxi to the station and come back for his car when his ankle had healed. Dashing on peachy lipstick, she marched downstairs. She was damned if she would withdraw in what he might well regard as abject surrender!

On the threshold to the kitchen Alyson nailed on a 'good morning' smile, but when she went in the room was empty. Although she was able to relax, her antennae remained alert, and a quarter of an hour later noises from above warned that Judd had risen. By now her breakfast was almost over and so, jamming a last spoonful of muesli into her mouth, she rapidly collected the dog's lead. A few minutes later, she was climbing the stile into the meadow.

When she returned, she found Judd eating toast and marmalade.

'Sleep well?' Alyson enquired, being determinedly pleasant.

'Fine.'

'How's the injury?'

He looked down the length of his blue jeans to where the denim was rolled up to reveal a damply bandaged ankle. 'Improving.'

'I heard you in the shower. Did you manage OK?'

'Yep.'

Alyson's lips compressed. After having been first bad-mouthed and then shunned yesterday, she had thought a night's sleep might have brought about a softening in his attitude. Some hopes!

'Very good at the concise answer, aren't you?' she snapped. 'I need to ring my office,' she continued, and with head held high she stalked out into the hall.

If some calamity had occurred which required her immediate presence, Alyson would not have minded. Indeed, she would have been revving up her car within minutes. However, her receptionist assured her that there were no problems and everything at Homeminders was running smoothly. She requested an update on various matters, they had a short chat, and within minutes she had returned to the kitchen.

'I take it you'll be digit-shuffling again?' Judd enquired, managing his first sentence of the day.

'Yep,' Alyson replied, in a tart tit-for-tat. 'After I've rehoused the gerbils,' she added, and promptly wheeled out on to the terrace and across to a range of outbuildings at the side of the house.

Trundling open the sliding wooden door, she entered what had once been a garage but which was now used as a dumping ground for the carpets, curtains and pieces of furniture which Gwen Brown's beautification programmes had made redundant. Here, on a melamine-topped table, the gerbils spent their summers.

'Such messy creatures,' her client had said, with a pained quiver of nostrils, 'but my husband bought them for Gary a long time ago and they refuse to die. I'd never have had the dog either, given the choice,' she had confided, heaving the sigh of the misused and overburdened.

As instructed, Alyson positioned the cage with fresh bedding close against the one which was currently occupied. All she needed to do, so Mrs Brown had explained, was open the new cage and slide up the bars of the old one, and the gerbils would run straight through. Then she closed the new cage and the transfer was complete. Easy.

She raised the two sets of bars and the first gerbil scampered over, but its companion proved to be more adventurously inclined. Halfway across, the animal abruptly twisted, leapt and knocked the cages apart. A split second later, it was slithering through the gap and leaping down on to the floor. Alyson gaped, realised the first gerbil might also make a bid for freedom, and turned to close the cage. When she turned back a split second later, the escapee had vanished.

With a mutter of dismay, she went and closed the door. Outside danger lurked in the form of wide open spaces and the Great Dane, and even though Mrs Brown might give three cheers she could not allow the runaway to actively seek its own destruction. Her eyes swivelling to left and right, she walked up and down. Beams of morning sunlight shone in through a side window, but the remainder of the garage was gloomy and switching on the single light did little to help. Where was the stupid creature? It had to be somewhere.

At last Alyson spotted it, beneath a rattan chair. She tiptoed forward, but as she came near her prey spotted *her* and skittered away. A chase ensued; the gerbil darting hither and thither with her in panting pursuit. Again it disappeared and, after another long search, again she found it—sitting calmly amid some rolls of carpet. This time when she approached, it did not move. Alleluia! she thought, but when she was a few feet away she suddenly halted. She shivered. Her skin crawled. The gerbil had a long thin tail and beady black eyes—it reminded her of a rat. Maybe it was patiently waiting and patently accessible, but she could not touch it. No way.

Keeping a sharp watch in case the fugitive should decide to scurry off again, Alyson opened the sliding door. Her teeth ground together. Asking for help from someone who was so hostile and so unrelenting went against the grain, but what other option had she?

'Judd?' she called. 'Judd? Can you spare a minute?'

She waited and soon he appeared, swinging towards her on his crutches.

'What's up?' he asked.

Alyson struggled to strike a balance between appeal and spirited independence, though it was tricky. 'I'm sorry to bother you,' she said, 'but one of the gerbils has got free.' She showed him into the garage. 'It's over there, see? It just needs picking up, but——' she cringed '—I can't do it.'

Judd forgot about being curt and stern-faced and instead looked amused. 'Who's a scaredy cat?' he enquired, in a sing-songy voice.

She was sorely tempted to hit him—hard—but instead she smiled.

'Would you put it back in its cage?' When he looked doubtful, her heart fell. He had to help her. He must. This far, Homeminders' record in pet care had been perfect. 'Please,'

Alyson begged, and then his mouth curved and she realised he had been deliberately keeping her in suspense. The rotter!

'You'll need to support me when I lean forward,' he told her.

'I'll hold on very tight,' she assured him.

Hopping over to the pile of carpets, Judd dispensed with his crutches. 'Both arms around my waist,' he instructed.

He bent. Alyson steadied him. His arm was outstretched and his fingers were clutching for capture, when the gerbil suddenly sprinted sideways. Judd made a grab for it and over-balanced. He grabbed for her and fell, toppling her with him.

'Whatever happened to you holding on tight?' he demanded, as they collapsed in a tangled heap of arms and legs.

'I didn't realise you were going to throw yourself forward,' she gasped.

They had gone with a whump! on the carpets, and it took a minute or two to recover. Lying there, imprisoned by his body, Alyson felt the thud of his heart against her breast and the sensual familiarity of his weight on hers. Her own heart started to thud. Inches from her eyes, curls of dark hair peeped provocatively from the neck of his shirt, and suddenly she was filled with the desire to touch them. She wanted to slide her hand across his chest and absorb the warmth of his skin. How would

Judd react if she did? she wondered. Would he order her to leave him alone and thrust her away? As he moved, his thighs rubbing against her, Alyson felt a spurt of satisfaction. He might despise her, but there was no disguising the fact that she still possessed the power to arouse him. His residual liking might have been cancelled out, but his residual desire remained.

It would serve him right if she unbuttoned his shirt and undid the black leather belt at his waist, she thought defiantly. And maybe she should unzip his jeans? That would teach him—— Alyson froze. In the corner of her eye she had seen a swift unnerving movement, but the next moment Judd's arm shot out.

'Gotcha!' he exclaimed.

The gerbil's furlough had ended.

'I'm going to have another cup of coffee,' Judd said, as they went back into the house. 'Want one?'

She cast him a sideways glance. He might not be granting a pardon, but the offer represented a small loosening of the strait-jacket he had placed her in and was not to be ignored. Besides, she fancied a drink before starting work.

'Please,' she nodded.

Judd switched on the filter machine. 'Tell me about your love life,' he said, as the coffee began to heat.

'Why?' asked Alyson, the demand taking her by surprise.

'Why not? Tell me about the blond bombshell.'

Her brows rose. 'You know about him?'

'The wife of a colleague rang me late one night, desperate to pass on the news that she'd seen you in a restaurant with one of the best-looking blokes she'd ever set eyes on,' he said drily.

Alyson sighed. 'The bombshell's name was Steven.'

'And?'

'I met him because I rent my office through his estate agency. We had a couple of meetings to arrange things, and I thought he was quite nice.'

'Only quite?' Judd queried.

'At that stage, yes. However, he wasted no time in declaring himself smitten and asked me out. He was so enthusiastic that—well, he swept me along, and almost before I knew it we were lovers.'

He spooned sugar into their cups. 'Did you live together?'

Alyson shook her head. 'I didn't want to, and——' she gave a wry smile '— Steven never mentioned it.'

'How long did the romance last?'

She pulled out a chair and sat down. 'Three months or so, until the day I caught him with a younger female.'

'Why are you so hung up on age?' Judd demanded. 'You're not only a hell of a long way from ancient, but also you happen to be one of the best-looking women *I've* ever set eyes on. Large expressive eyes, flawless complexion, and with those high cheekbones you'll keep your looks. You also have the kind of body that drives the male population wild. Personally, I——' He stopped short.

'You've finished?' Alyson enquired. He gave a brief nod. 'Then I'll continue. The female was six months old and he was pushing her pram.'

Judd's eyes opened wide. 'The guy was married?'

''Fraid so.'

He frowned. 'And he wasn't in the market of getting a divorce and marrying you?'

'When he realised I'd found him out, he suggested it——' Alyson turned down her mouth '—but I refused. You see, apart from the idea of breaking up a family being totally repellent, I didn't love him. Steven was bright, witty, appealingly confident about himself and about life, but he had a pathological aversion to telling the truth, the complete truth, and, deep down, I always knew it. He didn't just deceive me over his marriage, he acted the con-man on other occasions too.'

Judd poured out two cups of coffee. 'He sounds like a male version of your glamorous boss,' he remarked.

'Sophia?'

He nodded. 'She conned almost everyone she knew, including you and me.'

'She did? How?' Alyson asked curiously.

'To explain that, I need to explain about my relationship with her.' He cast her a glance. 'Which I should have done a long time ago.' He took a mouthful of coffee. 'To tell it in the right order—you'd talked so much about Sophia, the wonder woman, that before I met her I was cynical. I figured no one could live up to that kind of publicity. However, I was soon forced to admit that she possessed tremendous personal pulling power. She too was bright and witty, and although from the start I suspected she was one of nature's actresses and basically selfish, I found her good fun. Plus, initially the way she made it plain she found me attractive boosted my ego. I can be as susceptible as the next man to women drooling all over me,' he added sardonically. 'So when she asked for my advice on finance, I was all too willing to supply it.'

'That was how she conned you?' Alyson enquired.

Judd nodded. 'Sophia said she had a friend who owned a small import/export business and who was caught in a temporary cash-flow crisis. A short-term loan was required, but the bank were dragging their feet and the woman needed a quick alternative. Although this wasn't in my field, I spoke to some of my contacts and was able to provide Sophia with a list of commercial loan specialists, and as far as I was concerned that was that. I didn't say anything about it to you because she was very keen that our chat should be kept confidential and—well, it didn't seem important.' Judd took another drink of coffee. 'However, a while later she collared me again with the news that her friend hadn't had any success with the firms I'd suggested. I couldn't understand why, until Sophia confessed that the woman was in far worse trouble than she'd originally indicated. It turned out that, in addition to a huge overdraft, she was mortgaged up to the hilt and had no assets which could stand as security against payment of a loan.'

Alyson frowned. 'But if everything was in such a mess, surely a short-term loan wasn't going to make much difference?'

'That's what I told her. However, Sophia insisted all her friend needed was a slug of cash and she'd turn her business around. I said, sorry, but in her situation there was no way any firm would lend her the cash—any firm I could recommend. Sophia asked what I meant, so I explained that, of course, there are companies which will give loans against virtually no collateral but which charge astronomically high interest rates. Because she was hanging on my every word and because my ego responded,' he said laconically, 'I talked about them at great length and in magnificent detail. In particular, I told her about one notorious gent who'd lend any amount of money to anyone—at the right price.' Judd gave a harsh laugh. 'As you said, I never did trust Sophia, and I should have had the sense to keep my mouth shut.'

'She gave her friend the man's name and she negotiated a loan?' Alyson hazarded.

'It was Sophia who negotiated the loan, for herself. She waited until she'd signed on the dotted line and then cheerfully confessed.'

'Sophia had debts? The laundry was mortgaged up to the hilt?' she protested.

'Knocks you for the proverbial six, doesn't it? Her conversation, her manner, everything she did, implied success, and we knew her trade in your area was on the up and up. Sophia never gave me the full picture of how she'd landed in such straits, but if you think about it you soon realise that effect interested her more than efficiency, and she did nothing on the cheap. For example, her office was luxurious and in an unnecessarily expensive location, plus the cars she provided for her managers were renewed every year.'

'At my interview she said image was important,' Alyson reflected, 'and I think to her it was everything.'

'Damn near,' Judd agreed. 'Maybe if her profits had been ploughed back into the company everything would have been viable,' he continued. 'I don't know. But apparently the laundry was barely in operation before she began to siphon money off.'

'For what?'

'To upgrade her lifestyle. Although Trevor was a good provider it was never enough, and so she spent company cash on clothes——'

'She did dress well,' Alyson interrupted.

'Very well. When she said how much she spent on clothes annually I couldn't believe it, so she told me the price of just one of her outfits—and she could have paid off half Brazil's national debt instead! She used company funds to finance weekend breaks in luxury hotels while Trevor was away,' Judd went on.

'Weekends with other men?'

'I can't imagine her going alone or with a girlfriend, can you? And on paying for her domestic staff,' he completed.

'What domestic staff?' Alyson demanded. 'Sophia always reckoned she found housework no problem.'

'Ah, but did she say she did it herself?'

'I can't remember, but I definitely had that impression.' Her brows came down. 'Sophia also claimed her working day never allowed her a free minute, but that could have been a lie too.'

Judd nodded. 'When you consider the money she appeared to get through, it's clear she must have spent a fair amount of her time shopping. But that's what I mean about her conning everyone. By giving impressions—and making an impression—Sophia created a persona that dazzled, and when you're dazzled you don't see things too clearly. Her accountant must have realised something was fishy and yet as far as I'm aware he never demanded an investigation, so I can only assume he was dazzled too.' Judd gave an impatient sigh. 'But who am I to criticise? I should have told Trevor the source of the loan and explained that it was ill-advised, but I didn't. Instead I allowed her to dazzle me into believing she *would* turn her business around.' He frowned down into his coffee-cup. 'No, I'm kidding myself. The real reason I kept quiet was because I was afraid Trevor might hold me responsible.'

'Why you?' she queried.

'Because when Sophia told me she'd fixed the loan, she thanked me for giving her the man's name and implied that I'd done it on purpose because I wanted to help her. I quickly informed her that she was wrong—twice. First, because a loan on those terms was no kind of assistance; I could remember saying you'd need a mental age of three to take money on those terms. And second, because I'd simply been shooting my mouth off. Hell, I'd had no idea the laundry was in trouble.' He rested his elbows on the table. 'However, she wasn't having any. She stuck with her version and claimed I'd deliberately pointed her in the right direction. So, although I felt Trevor should be alerted, I hesitated because I wasn't sure whether he'd believe her or me.'

'But Sophia must have known you hadn't given her the information intentionally?' Alyson protested.

'She did. To begin with, I thought she was trying to place the onus of her actions on me because then she'd be able to blame me if it all went wrong, but later I came to the conclusion that she'd just wanted to inject a little male conspiracy. There was nothing Sophia enjoyed more than involving men in her life,' Judd added, in a dry voice. 'However, she fully understood that the loan was dodgy, and the only reason she took it was desperation.'

'I assume Trevor knew the laundry was in trouble?'

'He'd been told there were problems, though he'd no idea of their severity. And in order to keep it that way, Sophia needed him to believe that the bank had lent her the money in the normal manner.'

'This must have been what the two of you were discussing when I overheard you in her kitchen.' Alyson cast him a glance, wary of a belligerent reaction. 'The night I jumped to the wrong conclusion.'

Frowning, Judd rubbed a fingertip along his lower lip. 'It's a long time ago,' he said.

'You were complaining about how she'd tricked you and what a dangerous game she was playing, and Sophia talked about her happiness and how it was all due to you.'

'You appear to have total recall.'

'It was a traumatic moment,' Alyson said wryly. 'Sophia insisted Trevor mustn't know what had happened, or rather how it had happened, nor me either; because I'd be demoralised.' Her brows dipped. 'I'd be demoralised if I realised you'd provided the name of a loan shark? Hardly.'

'You'd be demoralised if you realised your beloved boss was not the successful businesswoman you imagined,' Judd corrected, exhibiting some recall of his own.

She grimaced. 'I was painfully starry-eyed.'

'But you thought you were supposed to be broken up if you discovered something about me,' he went on, 'and ten minutes later Sophia announced that she was pregnant and you thought that that was what we'd been talking about. What an almighty screw-up! If only——' Judd stopped. He looked at her and for a moment seemed about to say something, then he took a deep breath and rethought.

'Why didn't Sophia tell Trevor the truth about the laundry's troubles?' Alyson enquired, when he remained silent.

He roused himself. 'Due to a mixture of pride and shame, I suppose. After all, she'd failed with the business which he'd financed and which had been his idea.

'But she always claimed the laundry was her brainchild!'

Judd shook his head. 'Apparently Trevor felt she needed something to occupy her during his absences. Which, translated, means the fellow knew his wife liked to stray and was trying to find a way to stop her.

'How did you manage to stop her straying on to you?' Alyson enquired.

'With difficulty.' Piercing blue eyes met hers. 'You realise it was Sophia who made all the running?'

'Now, though——' She sighed. 'You were right, I can be blind where other women are concerned. But last night I did a lot of thinking and, looking back, I can see that Sophia considered herself a *femme fatale*—like Anne-Marie. That's why you were so wary of Anne-Marie, wasn't it? You recognised the type?'

Judd nodded. 'Straight away. I'd been normally and platonically friendly towards Sophia, yet, like Anne-Marie, for some reason she decided I was enraptured. Whenever she could she'd get me alone at her parties and flirt.'

'She'd clasp your arm and lay her head on your shoulder,' Alyson said, grinning.

'You noticed?'

'Yes, though I regarded it as play.'

'So did I—for a while, but then she began dropping heavy hints about us getting together. I tried to make it plain she wasn't my type, but——'

'Too old?'

'And too thin,' Judd said smartly, 'yet Sophia remained serenely immune. I think she believed she was irresistible. I should have been blunter, but she was your employer and you were happy in your job, and that made it difficult. I was worried that if I offended her she might get her revenge by firing you,' he explained. 'So I found myself trying to be amiable, while at the same time I kept her at arm's length. Not the simplest of tasks.'

'I wish you'd told me all this, and yet I know I'd have had difficulty believing it. I didn't believe Anne-Marie was making chase,' Alyson observed ruefully. She drank the last inch of what was now cold coffee. 'You remember you had lunch with Sophia,' she said, all of a sudden. 'Why go when you were so wary of her?'

'Because I didn't have much option. She rang me at the office and said she needed to discuss her friend's finances, and that she'd booked a table. She gave me the time and place, but before I could reply, let alone think up an excuse to refuse, the line went dead. Very reluctantly, I went along.' Judd's lip twisted. 'I reckoned I'd be safe in a public place. As we sat down to eat she revealed that she'd arranged a loan for herself,' Judd continued, 'and over dessert she suggested we should book a hotel room for the afternoon, and ... celebrate.'

'How did you refuse?' Alyson asked, intrigued because he had smiled.

'I told her I was very much in love with my wife and had no desire to fool around, but that, in any case, she left me cold. You see, by fixing the loan she'd given me the means to be blunt, because if she'd sacked you I'd have gone straight to Trevor and filled him in—regardless of whether he blamed me or not—and she knew that.'

'Sophia still kissed you in the kitchen,' she protested.

'As I said once before, there are some women who refuse to take no for an answer. I'd been congratulating myself on my escape, so when she suddenly grabbed me and thrust her tongue down my throat——' Judd gave an involuntary shudder '—I was too astonished to stop her.'

'The following morning I should have insisted on knowing what "nothing special" meant,' said Alyson, her tone full of regret, 'but I think the reason I didn't push too much was that I was scared of the things I thought I might hear.' For a minute or two, she was silent; engrossed in her thoughts, and her regrets. 'Did the loan enable Sophia to turn her business around?' she enquired.

Judd shook his head. 'There wasn't a chance.'

'So when you said she'd had an offer she couldn't refuse, you meant she was lucky to get what she did?'

'Very lucky. Trevor talked about the laundry when we met, and it appears things went from bad to worse. So much so, that by the time Sophia confessed all to him she was a whisker away from bankruptcy.'

'And when she confessed did she try to implicate you?' Alyson enquired.

'She never said a word. As soon as Trevor mentioned the laundry I explained how it had been me who provided the name of the guy who'd given her the loan, but although he hadn't known he wasn't interested. He said if Sophia hadn't got the money from there, she'd have approached some other cowboy outfit.'

'How did Trevor take the laundry's downfall?'

'He reckoned it had been one heck of a blow, but when I spoke to him he sounded amazingly philosophical.' Judd frowned. 'Now that Sophia's provided him with a child, I think he'd forgive her anything.'

Alyson cast him a look. Ever since she had sought his help with the gerbil, the atmosphere had been easier, but at his mention of the Carters' son his face had tightened. Memories had been triggered off, memories which, it seemed, had turned her into his enemy again.

Rising, she picked up their empty cups. 'I'll wash these and then I must get to work,' she said briskly.

She had filled the bowl and plunged her hands into the soapy water, when the telephone in the hall suddenly warbled.

'I'll get it,' said Judd, as she looked around for a towel and, fitting his crutches beneath his arms, he hopped out.

Alyson waited, wondering if she would be summoned, but no call came. The cups had been washed, dried and were back on their shelf before Judd returned to the kitchen.

'That was Mike Brown,' he revealed.

Her heart sank. 'What—what did he want?' she faltered.

'For a start he said he'd gathered I must be shacked up with some "homeminding woman" and he hoped I didn't mind.' A dark brow arched. 'I told him that, one way and another, we were having a ball. But the main reason he phoned was that he was anxious to talk to someone who'd been through a divorce, about divorce.'

Dismay shivered through her. 'Oh,' she said.

'You were right. Mike did attempt a pow-wow, and when Gwendolen proved unwilling to smoke the peace pipe he suggested a separation, but having progressed that far he's uncertain whether it's what he wants.'

'And what did you say?'

'I told him that forty per cent of those who do divorce are reckoned to regret it, and that their marriage should be worth something because they have a twenty-five-year backlog of commitment and——' Judd paused '—they share a son.'

'Was he aware Mrs Brown had played Jack the Slasher?' Alyson enquired, stalwartly ignoring any implications.

Judd shook his head. 'In the course of our conversation Mike mentioned that he'd spent Monday fishing, while his wife had been away for most of the day—visiting a cousin.'

'What was his reaction when you told him she'd been here?'

'I didn't.'

'You kept quiet?' she said, in surprise, then grinned. If earlier she had been tempted to hit him, now she wanted to hug him.

'I'm not sure I did the right thing,' Judd muttered.

'Thank you all the same.'

'Always pleased to help,' he replied drily.

Alyson tilted her head. 'You wouldn't be willing to help again? You see, although I don't have Sophia's financial problems, I am having a struggle with my tax return. Do you think——?'

'Lead the way,' said Judd.

CHAPTER EIGHT

EASY divorce was not a freedom, it was a trap, Alyson thought wistfully. Fifty years ago the laws had made a lot of sense, in that divorce had been so difficult, no one had embarked on one unless they were convinced it was what they wanted. She had not been convinced, she brooded—and now there were doubts about whether Judd's dedication to a split had been total. Indeed, she felt they had both over-reacted and that if they had put up a fight they might have won through to a worthwhile and permanent relationship. Alyson sighed. Neither of them had fought.

It was Friday morning and she was sitting on a bench in the hospital lobby, waiting for Judd who had been called in to see the doctor. The result of the examination, however, was a foregone conclusion, for each day the pain in his ankle had diminished and its strength had increased until now he was walking normally. Fretfully she twisted one of the golden gypsy hoops that hung in her ears. Soon he would emerge to inform her that it was goodbye. Soon he would disappear over the horizon. Soon she would be left to live her life alone—again.

Hazel eyes unseeing, Alyson gazed at the health posters that plastered the wall in front of her. She knew it sounded puerile, but the divorce proceedings had been in full swing before she had realised what was happening—after the abortion her mental turmoil had fogged out everything else—and when she had realised, she had failed to entirely believe. She had kept thinking that Judd must recognise they were making a big mistake and call a halt, or that their solicitors would instruct them to reconsider, or that someone—anyone—would order an attempt at reconciliation. No one had. Nothing had been done. By agreeing to a divorce she had set in motion forces which she had seemed unable to control, and the wheels had rolled relentlessly on. Something else she had found difficult to believe was Judd's failure to notice both her reluctance and her ongoing dejection. Yet maybe he had noticed, but had chosen to turn a blind eye?

Alyson fidgeted with the collar of the sea-green T-shirt she wore with blue jeans. Until a week ago, she had been certain her attachment to her ex-husband had been broken, but now she knew otherwise. Judd might tune her emotions to a higher pitch, yet it was only when he was near that she felt properly alive. All the reasons why she had first fallen in love with him remained intact. She liked the way he looked, his personality, his style. Instinctively she was in accord with the qualities he possessed. Alyson grimaced. It only needed basic intelligence to work out that the dearth of men in her life had been because, subconsciously, every one she met had been measured against Judd and found lacking. But it had not been just the men. Even the sensations of romance and the lovemaking she had experienced had been compared with her memories, to their disadvantage.

Restlessly she shifted her position. She remained hooked on Judd, but so what? Ever since she had confessed to the abortion, he had devoted a part of each day to contemplative silences, yet although she had longed for his change of heart it had not occurred. He might have completed her tax form and subsequently been an amiable enough companion, but no attempt had been made to dismantle the barrier which his fury had erected between them, nor had he come to her bed again. She squared her shoulders. Once he had gone she would pick up the pieces and carry on. She had survived three years without him, so there was no reason why she could not survive without him again. None. Her shoulders sagged. Survival seemed a poor consolation here and now. Indeed, it seemed like a living death.

The sound of footsteps broke into her reverie and she looked up to see Judd coming towards her.

Alyson leapt to her feet. 'All fit?' she enquired.

'Yep. The sprain's been officially declared healed and——' he performed a snatch of a soft-shoe shuffle '—I have permission to drive.'

'So now you're off back home,' she observed jauntily, as they headed for the swing doors.

Judd frowned and inspected his watch. Although his appointment had been first on the list, the doctor had been delayed and he had had to wait almost an hour before seeing him.

'I reckon I might as well hang on until after lunch,' he said, and cast her a glance. 'If that suits you?'

Alyson's stomach dipped. Whatever her feelings—*because* of her feelings—now that his departure had been sanctioned she was desperate for him to leave, and this delay would only prolong the agony.

She shone a wide Hollywood smile. 'Be my guest.'

When they returned to the oast-house, boisterous barks and much leaping around gave notice of the dog's eagerness to be exercised.

'I'll come with you,' said Judd, as Alyson reached for the lead.

Her stomach dipped again. She did not want him near. She wanted space between them. She *needed* space. His continued presence was playing a tantalising game with her equilibrium, and all it would take was one unguarded moment and she might disgrace herself by bursting into tears or, even worse, by falling at his feet and beseeching him to give her a second chance.

'Shouldn't you get packed?' she protested.

He shook his head. 'It won't take long. Besides, before I depart I'd like to get back in Rio's favour,' he grinned, 'and chucking a few sticks might do it.'

They locked the house and set off along the lane. High in the sky the sun was a glittering golden ball, and as they walked Judd unhooked the dark glasses which had been hung in the neck of his shirt and put them on.

'Why did you tell me about the abortion?' he asked, all of a sudden. 'There was no need. You could have kept quiet.'

Alyson shot a startled glance sideways. 'Because—because it seemed relevant to the conversation and because I felt you ought to know.'

'Why did you feel I should know?'

She frowned. She could not see his eyes and so it was difficult to gauge his mood, but it seemed possible that these questions could be the first shots fired in yet another attack on what he considered to be her wicked and frivolous decision. Her hackles rose. She had had enough of being abused, especially by a man who was annoyingly lingering when she needed him to go, go, *go*.

'I wanted to be honest and to clear things between us. I think I also had some kind of an idea that if I told you it would be . . . a burden put down. Shows how misguided us girls can be! I've admitted to short-sighted judgement and I know my perception of events was off-key,' Alyson went on, in a sharp metallic tone. 'I also realise that tolerance doesn't fit into your frame of reference. However, I resent you being so judgemental and I'm damned if I'll be harangued again! You won't believe this, but whatever the rights and wrongs something positive came out of the abortion—and out of our divorce too, for that matter. Every crisis contains the potential for greater self-awareness and growth, and Lucy made me understand that——' She lost patience. 'You can walk the dog—on your own!' she declared, and, thrusting the lead into his hand, she turned on her heel and began to march rapidly back towards the house.

A minute or so later Judd strode up alongside, dragging the reluctant Rio with him.

'Who's Lucy?' he asked.

She kept on walking. 'An abortion counsellor.'

Silence followed, during which Alyson was aware of the eyes behind the dark glasses subjecting her to a long and curious look.

'You consulted a counsellor?' Judd demanded.

She stopped dead and faced him. 'I did,' she said. 'I realise this isn't California and I know the British are supposed to come equipped with upper lips so stiff you can strike matches on them, but I found counselling immensely useful. If I had a broken arm I'd go to a doctor—you went to one with your ankle—so why not seek help from an expert when you have problems with the emotional side of life? You can mock, but——'

'I'm not mocking,' he interrupted.

Because Judd always seemed so self-sufficient, Alyson had automatically assumed he would ascribe to the school of thought which believed only the cracked or the cranky indulged in therapy—and now she subjected him to a suspicious scrutiny.

'No?'

Judd pulled his sunglasses halfway down his nose and looked gravely at her over the top of them. 'Not at all,' he assured her. 'Why don't we walk the dog—together—and you can tell me about this counselling?'

'No, thanks.'

'Aly, I'm interested,' he insisted. 'I should have been interested that morning when you asked about my relationship with Sophia, but I had other priorities. Wrong ones, as it turned out.' He gave a smile of entreaty. 'Please tell me.'

Alyson hesitated. Whereas earlier the abortion had made Judd uptight and furious, now he was calm. Maybe she should calm down too—and talk to him? If, before he left, he could be made to recognise at least something of how she had felt, it would be progress.

'All right,' she agreed, with a curt nod, and, much to the Great Dane's bewilderment, they turned and set off back towards the meadow. For a few minutes she was silent, gathering her thoughts, then she began to speak. 'A day or so after the operation it suddenly hit me that, no matter what I'd overheard in Sophia's kitchen, you had had nothing to do with her pregnancy. I can't say why, I just *knew*—and I was filled with galloping self-revulsion.'

'Because the abortion had been unnecessary?'

'It's more complicated than that.' Alyson gave a tight smile. 'But first let me explain about Lucy. As I told you, after the abortion I was miserable, then our marriage ended, and I realised I hadn't known what true misery meant.'

Judd frowned. 'The divorce hit you hard? I'm sorry if that sounds like a dumb question, but——'

'It does. The divorce nuked me!' she replied, thinking of how she had been unable to sleep at night and, during the days, had felt perpetually shaky and never far from tears. 'I was listless. I couldn't concentrate. At the office I was forever typing gobbledygook or filing letters in the wrong places or forgetting to deliver phone messages. It's amazing they didn't fire me.'

'You continued to work for the civil engineering firm you'd joined after you left the laundry?' he enquired.

Alyson nodded. 'I was with them until I set up Homeminders.'

'And you'd left the laundry not because you were bored, as you claimed, but because you believed Sophia and I were having an affair?'

'It seemed as if the affair was ending, if not already over, but I couldn't bear to have anything to do with her. In fact, I would have liked nothing better than to strangle the woman with one of her own damned ringlets! Where was I? Oh, yes, one day I noticed a poster in a local shop giving details of an abortion counselling group, and an evening or so later I found myself wandering in. Lucy was the therapist in charge.'

They had reached the stile. Judd unclipped the dog and it squirmed under the fence, while they clambered over.

'So you told her what had happened?' he prompted, as they began to walk across the grass with Rio following haphazardly behind.

'Not immediately. There was no pressure to contribute, so the first few times I just sat and listened to the other women—and to know my experience wasn't unique made me feel a whole lot better—but later I spoke to Lucy on my own. When she'd heard what I had to say she suggested I tell the group, so I did.'

'That must have taken some courage.'

Alyson gave a wry smile. 'Tons. Until then I'd bottled everything up, but although——' she made quotation marks '"talking things through" is trotted out as a general panacea these days, it does defuse things. It also forces you to take a long, hard look at yourself. You remember me saying that the backlash against you was just one reason why I had the abortion? Well, Lucy made me examine the entire rationale and acknowledge that although that and not wanting to bring a child into a one-parent family and so on were important, a part of my motivation—and probably the underlying cause of most of my angst—had been that I hadn't wanted a baby.'

Judd shot her a startled look. 'You didn't?'

'No,' she replied, and was relieved to discover that instead of the agitation which the abortion had previously incited, now she felt tranquil—and sure of herself and what she was saying. Perhaps telling him had been a burden finally put down, after all? 'You see, the cooking and the washing and looking after our flat had always loomed as massive and never-ending tasks, and——'

'If they did, it was only because you had such high standards,' he cut in.

'Agreed, but my lack of confidence as a housewife had raised doubts, albeit barely recognised ones, about how I'd manage as a mother. *If* I could manage.'

After investigating a multitude of smells, the Great Dane had come alongside and was looking expectantly up at Judd. In response, he broke a length of wood from a fallen branch and, with a heave of his arm, sent it winging across the meadow.

'Fetch!' he ordered, and Rio bounded off. 'You'd have managed fine,' he said.

Alyson shook her head. 'I think I'd have been so paranoid about the baby being clean and healthy and well fed that I would never have relaxed, and so the poor child wouldn't have been able to relax either. Then it might have cried and the crying would have worried me, and everything could have snowballed and become horribly fraught.'

Judd evaluated what she had said. 'I suppose it's possible.'

'Probable,' she asserted. 'I placed too much emphasis on perfection, and that was because I cared too much about what people thought. Especially what *you* thought—that was what all the housework was in aid of. I was desperate to please you.' She made a face. 'However, at the risk of being accused of spouting psychobabble, with Lucy's help I started on a process of self-discovery which began with my asking myself the existential question of "who am I?" and eventually ended with my having a far greater sense of *me*.'

His mouth tweaked. 'Which is why you're no longer happy to be my handmaiden?'

'Which is why I consider myself your equal!' Alyson came back with verve.

'Shouldn't it be my superior? You're the owner of a profit-making company, while my sole contribution to mankind appears to be dispensing missiles for the benefit of dogs,' said Judd, picking up the stick Rio had collected and pitching it through the air again. His expression sobered. 'Homeminders' success must give you a tangible sense of achievement,' he reflected.

'Very much,' she agreed. 'Setting up my own business and making it work is another of the positive things which came out of our divorce. When the smoke began to clear I felt a tremendous motivation to prove myself,' she explained, 'and it's great knowing you can support yourself and that you don't need anyone else to ratify your existence. But the beauty of being an entrepreneur is that I have the decisive hand,' Alyson went on. 'If I want a bigger business I can boost my advertising, or should I prefer a quieter life all I need to do is reduce the number of clients I accept.'

'Sounds the ideal set-up,' he observed.

'Obviously knowing my fear of inadequacy was the major factor in having the abortion didn't, and doesn't, fill me with pride,' Alyson continued, needing to complete her story, 'but in time I accepted it and found I could still like myself.'

'I like you, too,' said Judd.

She shot him a glance. 'You do?'

He removed his sunglasses and pushed them into the back pocket of his jeans. 'When you told me what had happened I felt as though something had been thrown at me very hard, and the only way I could handle it was by screaming. But in coming down on you like the wrath of God, I was out of line,' he told her, his blue eyes fixing on hers with total concentration. 'I gave no thought to what you'd gone through and I should have done. However, these past few days I've been thinking about . . . all sorts of things.' He stopped walking. 'Will you forgive me for being such a bastard?'

Alyson smiled. 'I will. I do.' She hesitated. 'I don't expect you to forgive me for the abortion, but——'

'Forgiveness isn't the issue,' Judd intervened. 'You were under pressure and you made what seemed to be the only possible decision in the circumstances, but, regardless of anything else, I consider it was your right to make that decision,' he declared, and there was utter assurance in his voice. He took a kick at a tuft of grass. 'Suppose we kiss and be friends?' he suggested.

The appeal in his eyes and his lopsided grin were difficult to resist, but Alyson knew that the touch of his lips against hers would be calamitous.

'I think a handshake will do,' she declared, with just a hint of a catch in her voice, and they formally shook hands.

Once more, the dog had retrieved the stick and lolloped back to deposit it at Judd's feet. Once more, he hurled it.

'You may have doubted your prowess as a mother, but I don't reckon I'd have been much good as a father,' he said, frowning.

'Too work-orientated?'

He nodded. 'I didn't give as much of myself as I should have done to our marriage, and it would have been the same if we'd had a child. I wouldn't have been prepared to devote enough time to being a dad and so both of us would have lost out.'

'Possible,' Alyson mused.

Judd's mouth took on a wry slant. 'Probable,' he stated.

The Great Dane returned and the stick was thrown again, and again, and again. In time they reached the end of the meadow, where they turned and began to retrace their steps.

'When you were talking about how desperate you used to be to please me, the implication was that you're not too interested in pleasing me now,' said Judd, and shot her a look. 'But you sure as hell made me ecstatic the other night, in bed.'

Alyson fixed her eyes on the distant stile. The mood had become far more comfortable but, first in suggesting they kiss and now by resurrecting their intimacy, he was overstepping the mark. She had no doubt that in the years ahead the memory of their illicit lovemaking was doomed to haunt her, but she needed no reminder now. Not from the man who had stood by and let their marriage dry up, crumble and blow away like dust.

'You'll want to avoid the rush-hour traffic, so we'd better have lunch soon,' she announced, and determinedly increased her pace.

For a moment Judd seemed about to protest, then he shrugged. 'You're the boss,' he said, and whistled up the dog.

Back at the house, Alyson launched herself into the preparation of a salad which would accompany cold poached salmon, while Judd went upstairs to pack. His estimation had been that it would take him a quarter of an hour, so when the food was quickly ready she went out on to the terrace. Restlessly she ambled around—soon he would be gone, soon—until she noticed the hammock still strung between the trees and decided to try it.

Kicking off her sneakers, she perched on the side and with a lift of legs, a swizzle and several wobbles, managed to install herself. Swinging horizontally in mid-air was a new sensation and, once the hammock had steadied, its feeling of cosy security surprised her. Hands linked behind her head, she gazed across to the window of the room where Judd was currently amassing his belongings. Would they ever meet again? she wondered. Did she want them to meet? Yes. No. She did not know. Right now, the only thing she knew was that she loved him and it seemed as though she always would. Alyson bit into her lip. The trouble with being a one-man woman was that, by definition, it made you a prisoner of love.

The warble of the telephone brought an end to her brooding, but provided a fresh dilemma—how did she get out of the hammock? She was debating the merits of rolling sideways and putting down her legs versus sitting up and jumping, when Judd shouted 'I have it!' from inside the house, and the warbling stopped.

Alyson lay back. Could this be Mr Brown calling again, she wondered, and, if so, what about? Had he taken on board Judd's warning about how often people regretted breaking up? She hoped so. Because it was at the Browns' house that the tragedy of her own marriage ending had been properly recognised, she needed theirs to endure. In a strange way, it seemed as if it would help redress the balance. Alyson gave up a silent prayer. Please, *please*, let Mr and Mrs Brown overcome their troubles and remain together.

A few minutes later, the kitchen door opened and Judd walked out across the terrace. In a blue open-necked shirt and jeans, and wearing battered brown boots, he looked so dear and so heartbreakingly attractive that a wave of love crashed over her—leaving a bitter-sweet ache in its wake.

'That was Mike,' he reported, as Alyson shuffled herself into a sitting position. 'It appears that this morning his wife finally confessed to being razor-happy, and he rang to ask whether or not we'd realised. I pretended we'd only just come across it,' he inserted. 'Mike demanded to know the full extent of the damage and—guess what?—when I told him he was not amused.'

Her heart shrivelled. 'Did he say if Mrs Brown was sorry?' she demanded.

'He said, and I quote, "She's full of apologies, but she can grovel till kingdom come and it'll make no bloody difference." So now he's determined to file for a divorce.'

'He mustn't!' Alyson protested, leaning forward in agitation and sending her resting place lurching. 'I'm going to phone him back. I know he'll say it's none of my business—and it isn't—but I have to persuade him to reconsider.'

Judd stretched out a hand to steady the wild swinging of the hammock. 'I've already tried,' he told her. 'I've repeated my earlier arguments, plus I've suggested that he and his wife should consult a marriage guidance counsellor.'

To know he was doing his best to rescue the Browns from a fate like theirs touched her deeply, and tears of gratitude rose in her eyes.

'Oh, Judd, thank you,' she smiled.

'There's no guarantee Mike will take my advice,' he warned. 'In fact, I'd be amazed if he does.' He frowned and for a long moment studied the toes of his boots, then he looked up. 'We should have sought help with our marriage,' he said.

A terrible sadness swamped her. 'Too late now,' she replied, in a high bright voice which sounded as if it belonged to someone else.

Judd's jaw tightened. 'You remember I spoke about a study which had been done on dealers? It also revealed that one in five has been divorced or separated. If I hadn't been so involved with my work, if I'd paid more attention to our private lives, then it might all have been different. I knew our closeness was beginning to suffer——'

'Because I was often brain-dead with fatigue,' Alyson inserted.

'Because neither of us left enough time for *us*,' Judd adjusted, 'but I ignored it. You see, I'd hit a run of failure at work. I know I never mentioned it,' he said, when she looked at him in surprise, 'but I enjoyed being regarded as a god, and the first rule in the handbook is that gods don't louse up.'

'But I can remember you saying that bad patches are inevitable,' Alyson protested.

'They are—sooner or later everyone falls foul; however, it was my first time. I guess all my life I'd been privileged in so much as things had never gone seriously wrong, so when they did it hit me hard.'

'When did this happen?' she enquired.

'The run began in the July before we split and, with the occasional remission, lasted for roughly three months.'

Alyson cast her mind back. 'Was this why you changed your mind about us starting a family?'

Judd nodded. 'Although I knew it wasn't, it seemed as though my career was hanging in the balance and I couldn't be bothered with anything else. I put all the other parts of my life on hold while I waited for my luck, my intuition, to come back.' He wiped a hand down his face. 'I did my damnedest to bring it back. Night after night, I worked myself ragged going through computer print-outs, studying the market, dissecting my disasters with anyone who'd listen.'

'And when I mentioned the evenings and you looked guilty, I thought you must be spending them with Sophia,' Alyson recollected.

'Which, in turn, led you to think about a divorce.'

She shook her head. 'When I suggested it that night, I never meant it,' she told him, and explained how she had been making a grand gesture.

'But I thought it was for real,' said Judd, and gave what looked like a surgically assisted smile.

'Whether it was or not, you were very non-chalant and totally accepting of the idea,' Alyson protested.

'On the contrary, I was stunned! But we were at a party and out on a veranda with other people within earshot, and it was the wrong time and place for what seemed like being a crucial discussion.' He gave an awkward hunch of his shoulders. 'Later, when I considered what you'd said, I didn't know what to do, so I decided that if I ignored it maybe it'd go away.'

'But you were the one who eventually instigated the divorce,' she reminded him.

'Only because you didn't appear to care about us any more, to care about me. Now I realise you were suffering from the aftermath of the abortion, but you became so withdrawn and sent out such strong "keep off" signals that I felt wounded and, in time, alienated.'

Alyson wanted to bawl. Although she knew her private melancholy had absorbed her, she had not realised she had been so unwittingly hostile. And just at the time when Judd's troubles at work must have made him long for tenderness and understanding at home.

'You thought I'd written you off?' she said rawly.

He nodded. 'I didn't know why, but it seemed I no longer appealed. Why else were you so quiet and remote? Why else would you let our marriage slip away? I agree you didn't actively push for a divorce, but you didn't do anything to stop it either.' He released a sigh. 'So often, I was on the brink of stopping it myself.'

Alyson's fingers curled tight into the web of the hammock. 'Why didn't you?'

'It was a combination of contrariness and stubborn male pride, I guess. I hadn't started the fire, so I didn't see why I should be the one to put it out; and I certainly wasn't going to go down on my knees and beg. But I still loved you,' Judd insisted, and the pain in his voice sliced through her. 'In those latter months maybe our verbal communication wasn't too good, but I made sure we continued to make love, and the physical contact was my way of letting you know that I wanted us to be close—and to stay close.'

'I wanted us to stay close too,' Alyson said, as tears well again.

'Then why didn't *you* do something?' he protested.

'Because I found it difficult to summon up the energy and——' she swallowed hard '—and because, at the time, being divorced seemed as though it was a fit and proper punishment for my having had the abortion.'

Judd gazed at her in horror. 'Aly, *no*. You don't believe that now?' he demanded.

She attempted to speak, but words were beyond her, so she gave a watery smile and shook her head.

'Don't cry,' he implored, reaching out to gently run his fingers along the curve of her cheek.

She swallowed again. 'For two supposedly intelligent people we certainly made a mess of things,' she said, and, despite all her efforts, her voice quavered.

'A hell of a mess.' Judd took hold of her hand and began toying with her fingers as though they were worry beads. 'I know there's a penalty to pay for everything, but I'd no idea the trade-off for my preoccupation with my career would be losing you.' A muscle moved in his jaw. 'I should have confessed to my failures, but I kept thinking I'd bounce back.'

'Which you did.'

'Eventually—and I began chasing the dream again,' Judd observed, with a brusque laugh. He gazed down at the slender pale golden fingers which were entwined with his own. 'Mike said there was no way he'd spend another night in the same hotel bedroom as his wife and that they'd be home early evening. So I thought I'd stay until they arrive and maybe we could both make an attempt to reconcile them. Mike's going to fiercely resent our intrusion, but——

'Good idea,' Alyson said quickly.

Listening to what Judd had had to say over the past few minutes, and especially to his talk of how much he had once loved her, had inspired the hope that—maybe—he could be inspired to love her again. And so it had become essential that he did not leave. Not yet. Alyson would inspire like someone demented, for letting their relationship end without a fight was not a mistake she intended to make twice. She would go all out, and if that meant throwing herself at him and making herself look silly, never mind. She was willing to relinquish all pride.

'Suppose you join me in the hammock and we plan our strategy?' she said, edging to one side.

Her suggestion seemed to take him by surprise, but he pulled off his boots and obligingly vaulted aboard.

'It'd be more comfortable if I put my arm around you,' he said, as they swung and swayed, and Alyson hastily agreed.

Discussing what to say to the Browns must wait, she decided, when her head was resting on his shoulder. What mattered was *her* strategy, and first it made sense to check that Judd was as unattached as he had claimed.

'You know all the women you've been seeing?' she enquired, being marvellously offhand.

He gave a derisive grunt. 'They were one big laugh after another.'

'Then you aren't... hankering after any of them?'

'No way.'

Alyson gave an inner cheer. So far, so good.

'You were talking about the other night when——' she took a breath '—I made you ecstatically happy.'

A brow arched. 'I was?'

'A while ago you were,' she said, blushing. 'I wondered, when you came into my room, whether your subconscious really did forget we were married or whether... I mean, thinking about it afterwards it did strike me as a bit far-fetched... though I suppose it might have happened...no, you couldn't have slid between the sheets unless...' She stopped, aware of tying herself up in knots. 'Was joining me in bed entirely innocent?' she enquired.

'No.'

'Oh,' she said, unprepared for such a prompt and straightforward answer.

'I wasn't intending to force myself on you, but——' the corner of Judd's mouth dimpled '—you could say I had roughly the same idea at the back of my mind as you have now, in inviting me into this hammock.'

Uncertain whether to protest her innocence or confess to her guilt, Alyson frowned.

'You're accusing me of having an ulterior motive?' she enquired, playing for time.

'I can read sub-text as well as anybody,' he replied, 'and that gleam in your eye is instantly recognisable. It's the one Anne-Marie had, the one which says you think we're made for each other.'

'And—and the one which scares the hell out of you?' Alyson faltered.

'The same.'

It seemed like a dead end. Where did she go from here? she wondered, in dismay. What did she say? Her colour deepened. Dispensing with pride had seemed far easier in theory than it was proving in practice.

'But I've been scared before,' Judd added, before she had a chance to formulate any words. 'I was terrified when we met again and I had a sudden sensation of unfinished business. Continue,' he instructed.

Having brought them into a cul-de-sac, he had, she realised, executed a swift three-point turn. Alyson's mouth twitched. She might have failed to read him properly in the past, but now she knew him well enough to know he was playing a game with her. And two could play games.

'Continue with what?' she enquired innocently.

'I don't want to sound like a complete idiot——'

'Pity!'

'—but I thought that, after telling me you loved me, you were going to try and sweet-talk me into marrying you again.' Judd looked down to the end of the hammock and wiggled his toes. 'Play your cards right and, who knows, I just might accept.'

'That's a bit much!' retorted Alyson, and reaching across him she yanked vigorously down on the side of the hammock.

'Hey!' he protested, as, with his free arm flailing, he clawed at the netting in a desperate attempt to stop himself from falling. 'Watch it!'

'And you, mister!' she retorted.

Judd hauled himself back to safety and re-established his position. 'I take it you're not prepared to grovel?'

'Well...' She took a breath. 'Maybe——'

'Suppose I do?' Judd suggested, and he gazed deep into her eyes. 'Aly, I love you. I've never stopped.'

Alyson felt a deep all-pervading joy. 'And I love you,' she said.

He began to kiss her with warm, eager, loving kisses. 'I know you reckoned it was too late for us,' he murmured, against her mouth, 'but——'

'Claptrap!'

He drew back, a sudden smile warming his face. 'So you'll marry me—again?'

'Yes, please!'

'Let's make it soon,' he said.

'As soon as possible,' Alyson agreed, then abruptly giggled. 'You realise everyone will think we're nuts? Marriage is supposed to be the triumph of hope over intelligence, but to marry the same person twice? That has to be——'

'You not only talk claptrap, sometimes you also talk too much,' Judd remonstrated, and his mouth came down on hers and he kissed her with a soft sensuality that made every nerve in her body tingle.

Alyson wrapped her arms around his neck and moved closer. She did not know whether

Judd was responsible or if it was due to being in the hammock, but as his kisses continued she succumbed to a gloriously heady sensation of floating.

'Remember I talked about chasing the dream?' he said, when he eventually found the strength to raise his lips from hers. 'Well, when it materialised—the success at work, the resultant promotions, the six-figure salary—somehow it was all like a fitted kitchen; it looked much better in the brochure.' He kissed the tender hollow at her throat. 'And that was because I didn't have you to share it with.'

'But now I'm here,' she murmured.

With limbs entwined, they lay there kissing and touching and caressing, and in time his shirt and her top were feverishly discarded.

'I can't take much more of this,' said Judd, with a groan. 'We're going to have to go indoors.'

Alyson rubbed her cheek against the dark hair on his chest. 'I thought you were joyously uninhibited?'

'You want me to make love to you in a hammock? Give me a break!' he said, in amused protest, and, climbing out, he gathered her up in his arms and carried her into the house.

The sheets were cool against her naked skin, but Judd's hands were warm, and as he began to caress her all over again Alyson quivered in hungry anticipation. He trailed his tongue around the edges of her mouth and she closed her eyes, submitting to the sweet torture of his kisses and of his hands. Seductively, he fondled her, and she recognised that there was knowledge of her in his long-fingered hands—and ownership.

Judd bent his head and she felt his dark hair brush against her breasts, then he was licking at her nipples, pulling and softly biting, on and on, until low animal sounds of pleasure filled her throat. A tide of need built, and his hand moved down her body to seek the moist opening at her thighs. Alyson shuddered as his fingers slipped inside her, and she arched towards him. Her breathing quickened. For dizzy minutes she submitted to the rapture he was slowly, expertly, relentlessly giving, but then, as she moaned again, Judd covered her body with his own. She arched her hips to take him in and, with a groan of pleasure, he buried himself inside her.

'Don't ever leave me, Aly,' he muttered, as their thighs cleaved together and they began to move in a sensuous rhythm—faster and faster, his thrust going deeper and deeper. 'Never again, never, never . . . *never*!'

CHAPTER NINE

THE following Friday afternoon, Judd carried out the box of papers and put them into the boot of Alyson's car. Her suitcase followed.

'Sure you've not forgotten anything?' he enquired, wryly eyeing the mound of her other belongings which sat on the gravel.

'Not a thing,' she assured him. Reaching down and in, down and in, she fitted everything else inside. 'I'd love to know how Gwen Brown managed to persuade her husband to stay in Warwick for the second week,' she said, as she straightened and slammed the lid, 'when he'd been hell-bent on coming home.'

'Perhaps she had a hammock handy,' Judd suggested, his blue eyes dancing, 'and perhaps Mike was inveigled into climbing in.'

'All I did was offer an invitation and—boom!—you were installed,' Alyson protested.

He wrapped his arms around her. 'And all you need to do is bend in your jeans and—boom!—the sensation is one of hardening of the organs.'

Alyson laughed. 'Again?'

'Even after seven days of gloriously intensive lovemaking.' Judd pushed aside the collar of her blouse and nuzzled his mouth against her shoulder. 'You don't think there'd be time for us to——'

''Fraid not. The Browns are due at any moment.'

He gave an impatient sigh. 'I wish they'd hurry up and let us get back to London.'

'You're anxious to start your new job as Homeminders' joint managing director?' Alyson enquired, her hazel eyes wide and innocent.

'I wasn't thinking along those lines,' Judd admitted. 'The weekend does come first.' He did not say it would be a weekend of gloriously intensive lovemaking. There was no need, the look in his eyes said it for him. 'I know it was your idea, but if you've had any doubts about me working with you,' he said, becoming serious, 'all you need to do is say.'

'I haven't.'

'OK, but if you should.'

'I won't. What about you?' she asked. 'Have you changed your mind?'

He shook his head. 'I think it's a great suggestion.' He laid his forehead against hers. 'After all, if, perchance you should wake up one morning and find yourself pregnant, then having someone who can run the show makes a lot of sense.'

'You reckon such an occasion may arise?' Alyson grinned.

'I think it could just be possible,' said Judd, with mock gravity.

She reached up and kissed the end of his nose. 'So do I. You really believe that the Browns have managed to mend their marriage?' she fretted.

'I really do,' he assured her. 'When Mike rang to say they'd decided to continue their holiday he sounded embarrassed, but a darn sight less irate, and the fact that there've been no further calls has to mean they're in the process of working everything out.'

'This time around we must tell each other our troubles and make sure we don't become victims of the rat race,' Alyson said earnestly.

His arms tightened around her. 'Same game, but different rules,' he agreed.

A moment later, there was a toot on a horn and they turned to see a white Rover swinging on to the drive. As Alyson stepped from Judd to adopt her professional Homeminders' demeanour, she saw that the two people in the car were smiling. She felt a swoop of relief, rapidly followed by pleasure. As she and Judd had joined forces again so, obviously, had the Browns. It was happy endings all round.

'There's a problem,' muttered Judd, as the car braked and doors began to open.

Alyson looked at him in sudden dismay. He knew Mike Brown well, so had he picked up intimations of disaster which she had failed to see? Were those wide smiles fakes?

'What?' she demanded.

He fingered his jaw in slow teasing deliberation. 'Do I introduce you as the first Mrs Hamilton, or the second?'

Alyson grinned up into his eyes. 'How about both?' she suggested.

Yours FREE an exciting MILLS & BOON —ROMANCE—

Spare a few moments to answer the questions overleaf and we will send you an exciting Mills & Boon Romance as our thank you.

Regular readers will know that from time to time Mills & Boon invite your opinions on our latest books, so that we can be sure of continuing to provide what you want - the very best in romantic fiction. Please can you spare the time to help us now, by filling in this questionnaire and posting it back to us TODAY, reply paid?

Don't forget to fill in your name and address - so we know where to send your **FREE BOOK**

See overleaf

JUST ANSWER THESE 8 QUESTIONS FOR YOUR FREE BOOK

1 **Did you enjoy Backlash by Elizabeth Oldfield**

Very much indeed ❑ Quite a lot ❑ Not particularly ❑ Not at all ❑

2 **What did you like best about it?**

The plot ❑ The hero ❑ The heroine ❑ The background ❑

3 **What did you like least about it?**

The plot ❑ The hero ❑ The heroine ❑ The background ❑

4 **Do you have any special comment to make about the story?**

____

____

5 **Age group:** under 25 ❑ 25-34 ❑ 35-44 ❑ 45-54 ❑ 55+ ❑

6 **Have you read more than six Mills & Boon Romances in the last two months?** Yes ❑ No ❑

7 **Would you like to read other books of this kind?** Yes ❑ No ❑

8 **What is your favourite type of book, apart from romantic fiction?**

____

Thank you for filling in this questionnaire. We hope that you enjoy your FREE book. Fill in your name and address below, put this page in an envelope and post it today to:

Mills & Boon Survey, FREEPOST, P.O. Box 236, Croydon CR9 9EL.

BACL

Mrs/Ms/Miss/Mr______________________________

Address__________________________________

____

____

____

Postcode __________________________________

NO STAMP NEEDED